T5-AFQ-176

SURVIVAL

EARTHQUAKE

For the women who taught us the meaning of courage:

Erma L. Kosanovich
Katherine B. Bale
Mary E. Peery

First Aladdin Paperbacks edition January 1998

Aladdin Paperbacks
An imprint of Simon & Schuster
Children's Publishing Division
1230 Avenue of the Americas
New York, NY 10020

Designed by Lily Malcom
The text of this book was set in 14 pt Bembo
Printed and bound in the United States of America
10

Library of Congress Cataloging-in-Publication Data
Duey, Kathleen.
Earthquake / Kathleen Duey and Karen A. Bale. — 1st Aladdin Paperbacks ed.
p. cm. — (Survival! ; bk. 2)
Summary: When two young strangers meet by chance on the day of the San Francisco earthquake, they struggle to survive the terror of crumbling buildings, fire, looting, and chaos.
ISBN 0-689-81308-2
[1. Survival—Fiction. 2. Earthquakes—California—San Francisco—Fiction.
3. San Francisco (Calif.)—Fiction.] I. Bale, Karen L. II. Title. III. Series:
Duey, Kathleen. Survival! ; bk. 2.
PZ7.D8694Eaj 1998
[Fic]—dc21 97-3578
CIP AC

SURVIVAL

EARTHQUAKE

San Francisco, 1906

K. Duey and K. A. Bale

Aladdin Paperbacks

CHAPTER ONE

It was almost dawn. Brendan O'Connor gripped the reins, struggling to control the nervous mare without slowing her down. Up and down Market Street wagon wheels gritted over the cobblestones. Drivers were hauling produce, laundry, milk, everything the hotels and restaurants would need for the day's business.

Brendan had worked hard to get this route and he wasn't going to lose it. His boss had the kind of temper no one wanted to set off. Two things made old man Hansen furious: losing money and late deliveries. Fancy San Francisco hotels like the Baldwin and thc Palace would find another bakery if their wealthy guests had to wait for their fresh-baked bread and pastries.

The street lamps had been turned off a few minutes before and the city was enveloped by a deep blue predawn glow. Brendan shivered. The damp early morning chill seeped through his worn woolen jacket. He looked up at the fading crescent moon. There wasn't a cloud in the sky. Maybe it would be warmer today. Still, he needed to find a better blanket for his cot soon.

So far, no one had objected to his sleeping in a corner of the furniture warehouse. Kelly Rourke, the night watchman at the warehouse, was happy enough to look the other way. When Kelly wanted to slip down to MacMurrough's to buy a whiskey, he'd shake Brendan awake to keep an eye on things until he got back. It seemed to be working out. Brendan hoped so. He didn't want to have to move for a while.

The mare pranced along even though the wagon was especially heavy today. There were three casks of olive oil Finelli's Restaurant was paying him two bits to deliver to the Palace Hotel. Old man Hansen would fire him if he knew Brendan was using the wagon to deliver other merchants' goods, but he needed Finelli's money. Every cent went into the leather pouch he had hidden behind a loose brick in the wall of Old St. Mary's Church. The pouch held everything that was dear to Brendan—his mother's wedding ring, his father's pocket watch, and the fifteen dollars he had managed to save over the last three years.

Brendan crossed himself and kissed his St. Christopher medal, then let it slide back down beneath his shirt. God would keep his money safe. He had gotten in the habit of hiding it when he was going to the mission school, back when his father was still alive. No one's pennies had been safe when Liam O'Connor had wanted a drink. Brendan had been on his own since his father had died—and it was better this way.

"May his soul rest in peace," Brendan whispered fiercely, as he always did to close off thoughts of his father.

The gong of an approaching cable car made the mare twitch her ears. Brendan pulled her closer to the curb and looked back over his shoulder. Dolan, a boy he had known most of his life, was whipping his team up Fourth Street, swinging a wide left turn onto Market. Brendan could hear the tall milk cans clanking against each other in the back of the high-sided dairy wagon.

The blue-uniformed cable car conductor shouted an angry warning. Dolan was already dragging at the reins, forcing his horses against the singletree as the cable car clattered past.

"Morning!" Dolan shouted, still grinning at the conductor's curses.

Brendan shook his head as Dolan got closer. "Hasn't Mr. Burke fired you yet?"

"Me?" Dolan retorted, reining in a little. "He couldn't run that place without me."

Cracking his whip, Dolan swung toward the center of the street. Brendan watched as the near-side horse struck its hoof against the tracks. It faltered but didn't stumble. Dolan leaned forward like an engraving of the old stagecoach drivers, snaking his whip over the team's backs.

Brendan faced front again. Dolan drove like a reckless fool, but you couldn't help but like him. It was too bad he hadn't been born fifty years before—he would have made a perfect freighter during the Gold Rush years.

The clatter of the cable car faded as it got farther away. Within an hour the United Railway cars would be coming up the middle of Market Street every few minutes. Brendan wanted to be on First Street by then, south of The Slot. He didn't trust the mare to stay steady once there were people dodging through the wagon traffic, running to jump onto the cars.

"Hey, Brendan!"

Brendan ignored James Walker's shout. Walker was a fast-talking dandy who wore cheap suits and was always looking for a free meal. Brendan had made the mistake of giving him bread once and the man had never forgotten it. Just behind Walker, a woman with her coat collar turned up against the chill made her way down the sidewalk. Her starched white hemline marked her as a hotel housekeeper. She did not look up as she passed Walker.

"Hey, Brendan!"

"Nothing extra this morning, Walker. Sorry." Brendan waved and slapped the reins on the mare's rump. She startled, lunging forward, and for a moment Brendan was afraid one of the oil casks would crash over, but it didn't. He dragged the reins back and the mare settled into her dancing walk. Brendan heard Walker's derisive laugh but refused to turn around.

At the Baldwin Hotel, the gray-haired cook made Brendan open every crate, checking the bread. "The crusts yesterday were like rock. I want them buttered." He looked up at Brendan. "These seem to be fine. But you tell Hansen if he shorts me on butter again, I'll be around to see him."

Brendan nodded. He was used to passing on the complaints—and listening to old man Hansen's explosive reactions. But Hansen always gave in, and he would this time, too. It was worth losing a few cents in butter to keep his clients happy.

Brendan climbed back onto the driver's bench. The sky was lightening. The first rays of sun struck the top story of the Call Building. At eighteen floors it towered above Newspaper Row—the *Chronicle* and *Examiner* buildings were big, but not as tall. Brendan liked delivering there. The newspapermen were always excited, walking the corridors, talking about Chicago, Paris, New York.

Brendan let the mare rise into a spanking trot. He sat up straighter, his chin high. He liked this part of Market Street. The buildings were smooth stone, their cornices elaborately carved. There were elegant triple-globed gas lamps. A few people were on the sidewalks now. The men wore suits of good, dark cloth, their felt bowlers tipped at jaunty angles on their heads. Some of them carried gold-handled canes. Most of them had heavy chains looped beneath their watch pockets.

The mare was still jumpy, but she stood well enough as Brendan hitched her to the iron post in front of the Call Building. Banjo, the old black gelding Brendan had driven when he first started, had never even needed to be tied. Brendan missed him, but old man Hansen insisted he use the mare now. She was finer-bred and made the freshly painted wagon a more impressive turnout.

Brendan opened the rear gate and leaned to slide the crates of mixed rolls toward himself. He stacked them three-high, then lifted them out, whistling to himself as he worked. The service entrance door stood open and Brendan went through.

The usual crowd of errand boys was waiting. They stood back to let him open the first crate, then swarmed forward. Brendan watched as they filled their boxes with rolls. When the first crate was empty, he moved it aside and opened the second. Clemmons, a tall, arrogant boy who annoyed Brendan, raised his usual fuss about the cinnamon buns.

Brendan nodded absently. "I'll tell Hansen you want more frosting."

"I've asked you to tell him that a dozen times."

Brendan didn't bother to answer. Clemmons took his share of the rolls and turned away, his air of self-importance dissolving when he nearly ran into Mr. Malloy.

Malloy was one of the best-known newspapermen in the city. He dodged around Clemmons, ignoring him, then smiled at Brendan. His handlebar mustache lifted to bare white, even teeth.

"Good morning, lad." Malloy half turned and addressed the crowd of employees. "Never known this boy to be late as long as he has been delivering here. He's a lesson to us all." People laughed and shot back good-natured gibes.

Brendan grinned. "Good morning, sir." He lifted the lid of the third crate just far enough to pick out the best cinnamon bun for Mr. Malloy.

"Ah, that's a beauty, all right." Malloy reached into his vest pocket for a nickel. "This is for your trouble."

"Thank you, sir." Brendan put the nickel in his pocket. "What news is there today, sir?"

Malloy shook his head, frowning. "Mine disaster in Calais, France. The report said over a hundred were killed. Terrible thing."

"Hey, Brendan, can you hurry it up? I've got to get back to the tenth floor or my boss will kill me." Cal Richmond stood anxiously next to the half-open crate. His blond hair looked nearly white under the electric lights.

Mr. Malloy smiled and turned back up the hallway, his polished boots clicking on the floor. Brendan watched him walk away, then turned to Cal.

"How many you need today?"

"A dozen ought to do it."

Cal was only a few years older than Brendan, but he was already a copyboy at the paper. Brendan liked him. Some mornings, they had time to talk a little. Cal wanted to become a reporter like Mr. Malloy. Brendan envied him. Being a reporter would be a lot more exciting than driving a bakery delivery wagon.

"See you tomorrow, Brendan?"

Brendan laughed. "Unless Mary McDermitt is right."

Cal smiled. "Mary McDermitt of the Flying Rollers—"

"—of the House of David," they said in unison.

When they stopped laughing, Brendan shook his head. "My father used to say there was always someone predicting the end of the world."

"He was right." Cal gathered up his boxes. He waved and started down the hallway.

Brendan counted what was left in the third box. He pulled his list from his jacket pocket and wrote how many rolls he had handed out so that Mr. Hansen could bill the newspaper at the end of the month. Old man Hansen would know if Brendan was off by even one.

Brendan scooped up the empty crates and hurried back out onto the sidewalk. The mare had shied at something and now stood kitty-corner in the traces. Brendan glanced upward. The sun was angling down the brick and stone buildings, working its way toward the street.

Brendan backed the mare around slowly. There was a little more traffic now. Up the street on the other side of the block, he could see a few men on their way into the *Chronicle* building. After hours, every whiskey bar within a half mile was full of newsmen arguing about politics and the state of the world.

A dark uniform caught Brendan's attention.

He nodded at Officer Kerrigan, then looked quickly away. He didn't want to answer questions about where he was living or how he was making out. Officer Kerrigan had known his father. Every policeman in San Francisco had known his father.

Brendan shook the reins over the mare's back. He had no time for daydreaming or dallying. His next stop was the Palace Hotel—the biggest and most important account on this route. Brendan loved the massive building, with its indoor courtyards and gardens. He had talked to several people who worked on the Palace grounds. They had told him about the fireplaces and toilets in every room.

Brendan looked up at the shining windows. Someday, he would stay at the Palace, a gentleman traveler with the taste and money to appreciate the fine wines and the hours-long banquets that included ten or fifteen elaborate courses. Someday.

CHAPTER TWO

Li Dai Yue walked with her eyes modestly downcast. She had not slept at all the night before. This morning she missed her cousin fiercely. Li Tan Sun was the only one who might have interceded for her, who might have talked to his father on her behalf. Dai Yue let her thoughts drift like ashes in the wind. It would do no good to mourn her cousin's death now.

Even though the sun would not be up for half an hour, the alleyway was crowded. The night workers were on their way home to sleep. Day workers hurried to the laundries and cigar factories. Houseboys with smooth, well-fed cheeks were beginning their morning trek to the Nob Hill mansions where they worked for *Fon Kwei,* white devil families.

Dai Yue watched a woman with lily feet hobbling with her walking sticks, her servants close behind. Deformed by years of tight bandages, the woman's toes were doubled back, her feet so stunted they fit into shoes small enough for a two-year-old baby. Dai Yue envied her. Her family would not marry her off to the first ugly old man who wanted her. She would be an honored bride.

As Dai Yue turned the corner onto Dupont Gai, the strong smell of roasting gingered pork irritated her nose. The street shops were opening up. She passed a wall covered with the usual sacred scarlet bulletins. She stepped around the men who had lined up to read them.

Through an open window she heard two men shouting, arguing over a *pai gow* debt. Dai Yue did not turn to look at them. Her uncle sometimes went to the Street of Gamblers to play fan-tan or mah-jongg—but he paid his debts. She could smell rose incense from a doorway. Demons hated incense. She slowed her step to let the odor fill her lungs.

A wagon pulled by a slat-ribbed mule creaked under its load of vegetable crates. The bright green of cress and bamboo contrasted with the rich colors of oranges and figs. Along the sidewalk, the butchers were hanging plucked chickens and ducks from sharpened hooks. Loops of sausages and gray-scaled fish lay displayed on tables where passersby could be tempted into buying them.

A breeze swept through the street, fluttering red banners announcing a wedding banquet and setting the wind bells into motion. Dai Yue looked up. Most of the balconies had chimes and flowered lanterns that swayed from silk cords.

Dai Yue slowed her steps to avoid brushing shoulders with a *boo how doy,* a fierce-eyed bodyguard who followed an old man dressed in heavy silk clothing. The old man looked neither left nor right, his long braided queue swinging with each step.

Dai Yue looked down the street. The balloon man wasn't on his corner yet. She loved the shiny balloons. They made her think of clouds and birds, made her dream of flying. If she were a balloon, she could drift with the wind out over the sea, maybe all the way back to Kwangtung Province. She had never seen her grandfather's house in the mountains, but her parents had told her about it many times before they died. There were steep canyons, many places to hide. Then she would never have to marry Chou Yee.

Dai Yue shook her head to clear it of disobedient thoughts. She saw a man looking at her and quickly lowered her eyes. She tried to walk faster, but the sidewalk was more and more crowded. Three men just ahead of her were deep in conversation. Their thick dialect was harsh and unfamiliar to her, impossible to understand. Perhaps they were from the lowlands, some delta fishing village in Choy Hung.

A cigar vendor's handcart blocked the sidewalk and Dai Yue followed the crowd, stepping into the rough cobblestone street to get around it. The vendor had just sold a cigar and was lighting it for his customer. The acrid, foul smoke streamed into Dai Yue's face as she passed. She turned away from it. Chou Yee smoked and his breath stank. His teeth were yellow and he was old and often surly. And in three years, when she was not yet sixteen, she would become his wife.

Dai Yue turned off Dupont Gai into a narrow street. Half a block later she turned again, this time going down an alley that led through to the Avenue of Virtue and Harmony. She crossed it, then turned again, dodging a wagon full of tall bamboo baskets overflowing with bouquets of lilies. Their fragrance eased her heart a little as she opened the door to her uncle's pharmacy.

Inside, her uncle stood at his long narrow worktable. He looked up when she came in, then back down at his work. His two assistants were busy preparing prescriptions. One had toad ashes spread across a white tray. Working with a tiny tool, he mixed the ashes with white powder. There were hundreds of drawers, jars, and bowls in the shop. They held tigers' teeth, snakes preserved in whiskey, horned toads caught in the California deserts, then burned to ash for rheumatism sufferers. There were green herbs and black tree bark and dried worms and centipedes. Dai Yue knew many of the medicines. Her uncle knew them all.

Dai Yue's uncle was chopping a slender black root into tiny pieces, working precisely, his hands deft. Dai Yue went to the back of the shop and ducked behind the shelves. The big preparation table was strewn with discarded stems and flecks of powdered leaves. The floor was filthy. She caught the sharp smell of ginseng root as she began to work.

Dai Yue first moved the *Mon War* collection box. She was careful not to touch the sacred paper, not to defile it. There was every kind of paper in the box—white and scarlet and gold. Lists, letters, and orders from clients. It held every scrap of paper that had been written on since the day before. She set the box down with reverence, turning quickly to startle any demon that lurked nearby. Then she opened the back door.

Dai Yue cleaned the tabletop, scrubbing it

with a bundle of rice stalks. She wiped the white stone pestle and her uncle's delicate balance scales. There was something sticky on the edge of his mixing bowl. It smelled sour, like meat going bad. Dai Yue wrinkled her nose.

She heard the doorbell jingle, then the voice of a Church Court footbinder. The woman wanted something to ease the pain of her clients' daughter's feet. The bandages had to be tight enough to stop the growth of the feet, to bend the bones under, and this caused great pain.

When the footbinder had gone, another customer came in. Dai Yue hoped this would be a very busy day. She did not want to talk to her uncle. The door jingled again and the *Mon War* collector came in. He emptied the box into his bag and left. Dai Yue watched him go.

She was sorry her uncle paid the twenty-five cents a month to have the sacred papers taken to the *Mon War Sher.* She wished she could have taken the box. She would have loved to have a chance to glimpse the joss, the dragons, the tigers of brass. The peanut oil lamps were said to burn day and night. Sometimes she saw the wagons filled with bags of sacred ashes as they left Chinatown. Someday she wanted to see the boats that carried the ashes out of the bay and gave them to the sea.

Dai Yue did her cleaning work as quickly as she could. She lit incense. Her uncle was very strict about keeping demons out of his shop and away from the medicines. As Dai Yue washed the floor, the door opened twice more and she heard her uncle's clipped, somber voice as he served his customers.

"Dai Yue," he called as the door closed behind a patron.

"Yes, Uncle?" She poked her head around the shelves.

He was walking toward her. "Is the table clean? Chin Loi will need to come back here soon."

"Yes, Uncle." She kept her eyes on the floor.

"Do not be sullen, Dai Yue. It is a pity you overheard the arrangements. I would have waited at least a year to tell you. But you will get used to the idea of marriage."

Dai Yue dared to look directly into her uncle's eyes. "Chou Yee is old. And *mean*."

Dai Yue's uncle stiffened his spine and glared at her. "The Chou family is making a fortune with its cigar factories. You will have a very good life."

Dai Yue looked down again to hide her eyes from her uncle. "I will not have a good life with that man." She clenched her fists.

"You are young and very foolish, niece. No girl knows what is best for her."

Dai Yue fought to control the feelings that boiled like a rice pot inside her. Her uncle stepped forward to grip her shoulder and she moved back, shrugging his hand away.

"I do not wish to marry Chou Yee," Dai Yue whispered.

Her uncle reached for her hands. "Oh, but you will. And one day you will thank me for arranging so good a marriage."

Dai Yue glanced out the back door. The sky was lightening. It would be a sunny day.

"There will be many customers today, Dai Yue. Finish your work." Her uncle turned on his heel, the thick white soles of his black slippers making no sound as he walked away from her. Dai Yue stared after him, tears stinging her eyes. Her uncle glanced back at her and his frown deepened. "You have no time to waste with foolish tears. Now finish your work."

Without knowing she was going to do it, Dai Yue found herself spinning around, reaching for the back door.

"Dai Yue!"

Her uncle's shout seemed to push her out the door. She stood blinking in the grayish light of dawn.

"Dai Yue!"

She began to run.

"Chin Loi!" her uncle screamed from behind her. She heard the door open, the footsteps, her uncle's muttered orders to his young assistant. Then she turned a corner and heard nothing at all.

Dai Yue ran without thinking, without looking back, dodging through the throngs of men. She pounded up an alley, then turned into a narrow street she knew led back to Dupont Gai.

"Li Dai Yue? Wait! Come back!" Chin Loi called from behind her.

Dai Yue ran faster, sliding around the corner onto Dupont Gai. Here, even at this early hour, the crowds were so thick she had to slow her pace. Frantically, she worked her way sideways, crossing the street. She was careful, glancing back, keeping as many people between herself and Chin Loi as she could. She caught a glimpse of him as she jumped up on the sidewalk. He was looking left and right. He had lost her.

Dai Yue began to run again. She jostled a porcelain vendor setting up his wares. He shook his fist at her and she glanced back. Chin Loi had not given up. He had spotted her. Apologizing to the vendor, Dai Yue speeded up again, this time veering back into the street, hoping she could get away, find a place to cry, to calm down.

"Dai Yue! You must slow down, your uncle—"

Chin Loi's words were cut off by the rumbling of a produce wagon on the uneven cobblestone.

Dai Yue glanced over her shoulder. Chin Loi was closer. Much closer. His face was flushed and angry. The produce wagon blocked Dai Yue's way. Frantic, she pulled herself up onto the back edge of the wagon. She rolled against a crate of cabbages, hearing her tunic tear on the rough slats.

"Dai Yue!"

She turned away, her breathing ragged and painful, unable to hold back her tears any longer. There was a heavy canvas draped over the crate. Dai Yue pulled at it, covering herself like a little child, hiding her face and her tears. She expected any second to feel Chin Loi's hands on her shoulders, to hear his harsh voice. But she did not.

For a long time, Dai Yue wept. It was wrong that her uncle would give her to someone like Chou Yee. It was unfair that her father and mother had died. Her tears of anger cooled into tears of grief. Li Tan Sun, her beloved cousin, had been the only one to stand up to his father. He had refused to bow his head before anyone.

Dai Yue wiped at her eyes. Tan Sun's pride had

been the cause of his death. He had attended the Chinese Mission school, had learned the strange, ugly English words. He had taught her, too, making her repeat the phrases over and over. He had made friends among the Fon Kwei, or so he thought.

Then, one drunken night, Tan Sun's friends had turned on him like animals. They had cut his queue and beaten him senseless and left him bleeding in the street like some discarded piece of trash.

The wagon bed rose, then dropped, jarring her badly. Her cheek struck the wood and without meaning to, she started crying again. When Dai Yue finally looked out from beneath the canvas, she caught her breath.

On either side of the street, buildings rose into the sky, much higher than any building in the City of the Sons of Tang. How strange that all this existed so close to her home and she had never seen it. The buildings were so tall Dai Yue could scarcely understand why they did not fall over. Ornate decorations, carved from what looked like stone, covered the fronts and corners of the buildings. Dai Yue pushed the canvas back a little farther. The streets were bustling, a cable car gong sounded somewhere ahead. Polished gas lamps graced the sidewalks.

Loud feminine laughter made Dai Yue sit up, astonished, smoothing her tunic. Four women in heavy, draped skirts and strange hats were walking, their arms linked. Their eyes were not lowered. One was gesturing, her right arm raised above her head, her parasol dangling from her wrist as she laughed again with her companions.

Dai Yue had heard of this. Every seven years, on the Festival of the Good Lady, the women of Chinatown were allowed to explore, strolling the streets as freely as men for a single day. Some even left Chinatown. Her upstairs neighbor had often told the stories of the bold Fon Kwei women and their careless public behavior.

"You! What are you doing there?"

Dai Yue jerked around to see the wagon driver glaring at her. He cursed and reined in. Dai Yue scooted to the edge of the wagon bed and jumped off. She ran, and heard the driver's angry shouts fade behind her.

Out of breath, Dai Yue slowed to an uneasy walk, trying to take in the vast wideness of the street. She wasn't sure how to get home. The sky was gray blue now, glowing with the coming of dawn. There were men in dark clothes, carrying polished walking sticks in their hands, their mustaches and beards as full and bristling as animal fur. She could hear the odd, soft-shaped words of the Fon Kwei. She could make sense out of some of the talk, but it frightened her to hear so much of it, to be surrounded by the strange, foreign voices.

"Hey! Girl!"

Dai Yue whirled to see a red-faced Fon Kwei coming toward her. He was tall, his florid face crowned by orange hair. There were tiny patches of brown scattered across his cheeks, speckling his skin.

Backing into the street, Dai Yue froze with fear. Hoofbeats and a shout made her turn. She had stepped in front of a wagon driven by a boy about her age. The boy stood up to haul backward on the reins, pulling his horse to a stop inches from her.

The boy jumped down from the wagon. "Are you all right?"

Dai Yue was silent. She understood his words and she could have answered him, but her voice seemed like a jagged thing, caught low in her throat.

"Are you hurt? I—"

The boy's words were interrupted by an eerie, rolling roar that seemed to come from the very earth itself.

CHAPTER THREE

Brendan turned from the Chinese girl. He faced the low rumbling that seemed to roll in from the sea, roaring up Market Street, a groaning that sounded like Hell had been set loose. Without thinking, Brendan reached for his St. Christopher medal and held it so tightly it dug into his palms.

The cobblestones beneath Brendan's feet slammed impossibly to one side, then back. The mare reared, her eyes ringed with white. Brendan grabbed the Chinese girl and dragged her out of the way, stumbling, pulling her down with him as he fell. The mare struck at the ground, then lunged forward. She galloped past, taking a mad, zigzagging course down Market.

The wagon narrowly missed an automobile. The driver shook his fist at Brendan.

The street was heaving up and down, as though the earth had somehow become water, rocked by violent waves. Brendan heard screams from the Palace Hotel; the windows were shattering, a deadly rain of glass falling onto the broken cobblestones. Brendan fought to stand, but the ground moved beneath his feet and he fell again. The Chinese girl sat motionless. Her eyes flickered from one building to the next, her lips moving in a whisper Brendan knew he would not understand even if he could hear her over the demonic roaring of the earth.

The groaning roar went on as Brendan faced westward down Market Street. The Call Building shivered and swayed, writhing against the sky. Bricks exploded from their mortar and Brendan watched one fall, then disappear against the dark building. Dozens of reporters and copyboys shoved their way into the street. Brendan thought he recognized Cal Richmond. He was staggering, both hands pressed to his head. Blood darkened his light hair.

"Help me! Help me!" A woman ran toward them. She wore only her nightclothes. Her bare feet were cut and bleeding. There were long scratches across her face. Her eyes were wild and she lurched, trying to keep her balance on the heaving ground. She scowled at Brendan, then went on.

Brendan heard a clatter of bricks striking the cobblestones close by. He tried to stand up, struggling against a mysterious weight. He looked down, horror-stricken, only to realize that the Chinese girl had taken hold of his hand. Her eyes were blank with fear, her hand a claw, clutching his own.

"Get up," he shouted at her. "The buildings are going to fall!"

She only stared, not even blinking. The ground beneath them shivered, the waves coming closer together. A party of nightgowned women fled past. Brendan squinted, confused for a second. They all seemed to be wearing red shoes. Their bare feet were bleeding, every one of them cut badly on the carpet of shattered glass from nine stories of broken windows.

"Get up," Brendan screamed again, jerking the Chinese girl upward, staggering back as he dragged her to her feet. Her face was pale in the early dawn light. Brendan heard a sharp hissing sound from above. He looked up. Eerie blue-green sparks arced and spat. The electric lines had broken. A chorus of shrill, high-pitched shrieking made Brendan lower his eyes to look across the street again.

People were pouring out of the Palace Hotel now. A milling crowd of half-dressed men and women clogged the sidewalk and spilled into the street. A small dog stood stiff-legged, barking frantically at them as though they had somehow caused its world to go crazy. The Chinese girl shrank against Brendan.

Then, without warning, as abruptly as it had begun shaking, the ground became still. The crowd in front of the Palace stopped. Screams faded. People stood rigidly, as if afraid that any motion, any sound, would be dangerous. Overhead, the blue sparks cracked like distant gunfire.

Brendan looked into the Chinese girl's frightened eyes. "Are you all right?"

She opened her mouth as if to answer, but in that instant another convulsion slammed through the layers of soil and rock beneath the city. The Chinese girl tightened her grip on Brendan's hand. Together, they managed to keep their feet this time as the buildings quivered, then resumed their deadly swaying dance. The steel beams that formed the skeletons of the brick buildings were shrieking as the ground writhed.

Brendan stumbled against the girl. She pointed, her eyes glazed with fear. He followed her gesture and blinked, trying to clear his vision. Dust was billowing between the buildings and at first he could not believe his eyes.

The cable car tracks were twisting, arching themselves into loops and curves. As Brendan watched, the ground along the tracks began to split apart. The Chinese girl stared at it.

Brendan tried to move, tried to run, but he could not. He stood riveted as the crack in the earth widened, like a seam splitting. It raced toward them and the girl froze. Brendan fought the heaving motion of the ground, pulling her backward.

A sudden sideways jolt knocked them both down again. Brendan scrabbled away, weak with fear, whispering frantic prayers to the Virgin Mary. Without thought or intent, he dragged the Chinese girl with him, his grip on her hand tightening as his panic rose.

The crack lengthened like a snake crawling toward them. The girl managed to gain her feet, pulling him upright, jerking him into a clumsy retreat through the hellish roar of falling brick and collapsing steel.

A cold, piercing pain just above Brendan's right eye made him stumble, but the girl kept him on his feet, kept him running. They wove through the crowd, assaulted by moans, prayers, and shouts of fury. One man shook his bloody fist at the sky, accusing God. Beside him another man knelt, weeping and begging someone to show him how to pray.

Brendan followed the girl around a pile of bricks and shattered wood. A second later he was sliding, running across a spilled load of oranges. He saw the wagon, tilted, one wheel broken. The driver lay sideways on the bench, his forehead bloody, his eyes closed. One of the horses had fallen. It looked dead. Its harness mate stood breathing hard, trapped in the tangled leather.

The Chinese girl yanked at Brendan's hand and he realized he had stopped. In that instant, the world became still again. The insane motion of the street quieted and the crowds hushed. Dust hung in the air, smudging the rising sun with yellow and orange.

Brendan let go of the girl's hand and turned in a slow circle. His thoughts were too loud, hammering against his skull. The silence in the street seemed to swell, pressing against the buildings, flowing upward with the dust that drifted skyward, enveloping the city. It rang in Brendan's ears, immense.

Brendan shook his head and rubbed one hand over his face. The stickiness of his own blood startled him. He stared at his fingers, amazed at the glaring red.

Dai Yue stood still, feeling as if the sudden silence had taken them all in its arms. The ground was no longer moving, had stopped its terrible shaking, but she was afraid to take a step, afraid she would rouse Day Leong again. The Earth Dragon had already shown his rage.

The sound of bricks striking the cobblestones made her spin around. She saw two more fall, hit the street, bound up once, then roll to a standstill. A tiny murmur ran through the motionless crowd, then the silence closed in once more. The dust was thick. It was hard to take a deep breath.

Dai Yue glanced at the Fon Kwei boy. His already pale face was an ugly white, streaked with blood running from a cut on his temple. Dai Yue looked down at her tunic. It was old, a castoff from a neighbor's daughter, mended and faded. She pulled at the hem, her thumbs close together on the cloth, until she managed to start a tiny tear. She ripped a strip from around the hem. With the cloth dangling from her hand, she faced the Fon Kwei boy.

"Are you all right?" he asked her when he saw her looking at him.

Stupid, Dai Yue thought. He was bleeding, but he asked, yet again, if she was hurt. The Fon Kwei had no brains, no matter what her cousin had said about the teachers at St. Mary's Mission School.

"You hurt," Dai Yue managed.

His face lit instantly. "You speak English!"

She lowered her eyes, almost blushing at his earnest foolishness. He was looking at her as if she were a horse or a dog that had suddenly acquired human speech. All doubts were gone. Fon Kwei were idiots. "Not too much," she answered modestly. She lifted the strip of her tunic, gesturing at his wound.

"I'm bleeding pretty hard," the boy said, nodding.

Dai Yue motioned for him to sit down. She bandaged him as well as she could, tucking under the end of the cloth strip. As she worked, her fingers began to tremble. She kept glancing up at the buildings, imagining for a split second that she could see them move.

"Look at this." The Fon Kwei boy held out his hands. "I'm shaking."

Dai Yue clasped and unclasped her own hands. "I, too."

The Fon Kwei boy looked around, his eyes searching. A second later Dai Yue realized what had made him turn. Somewhere, someone was crying. The crowd had begun to move again, aimless, dreamlike.

The sea of Fon Kwei faces made Dai Yue uneasy. None of them seemed to notice her, but Dai Yue knew it was only a matter of time before someone did. Chinese men rarely ventured out of Chinatown unless they worked for Fon Kwei families. Chinese girls of good family were never seen in public like this.

Involuntarily, Dai Yue looked down at her clothes. Her slippers were soiled, dirt clinging to the heavy black cloth. Her trousers and tunic were filthy, smudged with blood. It was his, Dai Yue realized. Fon Kwei blood.

Dai Yue's thoughts spun in a circle and made her dizzy. Had the boys who had beaten her cousin to death been spattered with his blood?

Had they washed it off or worn it with pride? She shivered with hatred.

"Are you all right?" The Fon Kwei boy asked again.

"No," Dai Yue snapped at him.

"Are you hurt?"

Dai Yue glared at him.

"What's your name?"

Dai Yue hesitated. She had never given her name to a Fon Kwei—not even the policemen who sometimes came into her uncle's pharmacy to ask questions about opium or some mysterious poison they had found. Dai Yue's uncle knew every mushroom, every snake's venom, every bitter herb that could cause illness or death—many of these things, in tiny doses, acted as cures.

The Fon Kwei boy was studying her face. "My name is Brendan O'Connor."

Dai Yue looked at him sidelong. What did she care about his name? "I go," she began, then stopped, searching for the right word. "I go . . . home."

His face changed. "I'll go with you."

Dai Yue looked aside. "No. I go alone."

The boy reached for her hand. Before she could react, he had taken it and was looking into her eyes. "You can't. It's too dangerous." He gestured, taking in the stunned crowds, the broken glass, the piles of brick and wood in the street.

Dai Yue stepped back, pulling her hand free from his. "You go home now?"

The boy shook his head. "The only place I need to go is to St. Mary's. You know it?"

Dai Yue nodded. "The Fon Kwei church?" The words felt awkward and misshapen in her mouth.

The boy looked puzzled. "What's your name?" he repeated.

"Li Dai Yue. Dai Yue," she repeated, just as the earth shook beneath them once more.

The throng of people around them froze in place. Women screamed and one of the men who had been praying began to curse. Dai Yue felt the coldest fear of her life grip at her heart. Was the Earth Dragon going to destroy the whole world? The boy reached for her hand and she gave it to him. Together they stood waiting, holding their breath, until the tremor ceased.

"I hate this," the boy whispered. He clutched at a silver chain around his neck.

Dai Yue had seen the silver coin that hung from it. It meant something to the Fon Kwei boy, that much was very clear. His lips moved a little. Prayer?

A shower of bricks and chunks of broken mortar fell into the crowd. A woman howled in pain. "I want to go home," Dai Yue said, without meaning to.

Somehow, in the noisy confusion, the boy heard her. He began walking away from the rising sun, leading her through the broken glass, the people who wandered in blind, terrified circles.

CHAPTER FOUR

At first, Brendan walked slowly. His legs felt different, longer, as though his light, confused thoughts were a mile above his feet. The bandage Dai Yue had wrapped around his wound was tight. He could feel his pulse pushing at the cloth.

There was a strange odor in the air, something that lay beneath the smells of dust and powdered mortar. The heavy silence was now broken with screams and pleas for help on all sides. The voices seemed to drift into Brendan's ears, then out again. He could make no sense of anything. It felt as though there were a pane of glass between himself and the world. A quick pressure on his hand reminded him that Dai

Yue was walking with him through the nightmarish street.

The crowd thickened as they passed the Call Building. Brendan glanced at Dai Yue. Her eyes were full of fear, skittering across the faces closest to them.

"Hey, look out, boy!"

Brendan found himself facing a tall, dark-haired man. "I'm sorry, sir."

"You should be. You. . . ."

Brendan watched the man's eyes shift from him to Dai Yue. He felt her hand tighten on his.

"What's this girl doing here? She belong to you?"

Brendan glanced at Dai Yue. Her eyes were empty, bottomless. Brendan couldn't tell if she had understood the man.

"I asked you a question, boy."

Brendan hesitated. So many Chinese girls were slaves, were forced into prostitution. The man was still staring at Dai Yue. Her eyes were downcast and her face was unreadable. But Brendan felt her tighten her hand on his once more, and she was trembling again.

"Yes," Brendan almost shouted at the man. "She belongs to my family. She helps our cook."

The man looked back at Brendan, taking in his worn jacket, his patched trousers, and his thin-soled shoes. "Who's your father?"

Brendan mumbled something, pulling Dai Yue forward and to the side. He walked fast, weaving his way through the shouting men, Dai Yue so close behind him that she kept stepping on his heel.

"Malloy!"

Brendan searched for the source of the shout.

"Malloy! James! Thompson!"

It was a gray-haired man standing almost in the center of the broad street, between the cable car tracks. As Brendan watched, Mr. Malloy and two other men responded to the shout. They stood in a loose circle and Brendan could hear the gray-haired man's words.

"Fires are spreading. Hopper is already out there somewhere. Find out the origins and extent of the fires, and if you can ascertain the direction they are spreading, maybe we can help the police and the firemen. Whole sections of the city are going to have to be evacuated."

Brendan felt Dai Yue tug at his hand. "Fire?"

Brendan nodded slowly, noticing for the first time the faint smell of smoke in the air. He pictured the three enormous ovens at old man Hansen's bakery. If the earthquake had upset them, there would be coals scattered across the plank floor right now, eating their way into the wood.

A soft hissing sound caught Brendan's attention. He ignored Dai Yue's insistent glare to focus on it. *Gas,* he thought, his stomach tightening. The gas lines had been broken.

"Is that you, O'Connor?"

Mr. Malloy's voice startled Brendan. "Yes, sir?"

The tall, mustached man gripped his shoulder. "It isn't safe here, son. The fires will likely come this way." His gaze shifted to Dai Yue. "And you should get this young lady back to her home. People are a little on edge right now."

Brendan nodded, but Mr. Malloy was already

striding away. A motion across the street caught Brendan's eye. On the second story a dentist's sign swayed. A second later, Brendan felt the earth beginning to move again.

The crowd fell silent. Men gazed at the sky or gaped at the cobblestone beneath their feet. Brendan felt his heart race. The tremor loosened a few bricks, which crashed to the street. Then it faded. Church bells all over the city rang three or four times, then stopped.

Brendan glanced at Dai Yue. Her glare had softened into a dazed expression. She followed without resistance when he led her forward. There was less rubble in the street here. The cable tracks were undamaged.

A woman pushing a pram jammed with alabaster statues and a oval gilt mirror passed them, nearly running. Her dressing gown was stained and torn. Her face was smudged. Her expression mirrored the faces around her. She looked stunned, unsure of everything.

Brendan guided Dai Yue up onto the sidewalk at the corner of Dupont Street. A man dragging a heavy trunk nearly ran into them.

He did not apologize. He barely looked at them. A cart horse lay dead in the street and Brendan glanced away, thinking about Hansen's mare. Maybe he should have chased her down Market. What would he tell old man Hansen? Would he ever see him again?

"I want to go home," Dai Yue said, pulling him to a halt.

"That's where we're going," Brendan told her. He pointed. Dupont Street rose steadily toward Chinatown. "I have to go to St. Mary's, then I'll help you get back to your family." He watched her face. It had gone blank again. A sudden thought occurred to him. "Don't you have a family?"

Dai Yue frowned. "One uncle."

Brendan took a deep breath. He could smell smoke more strongly now, he realized. "I have to go to—"

"No. I want to go home," Dai Yue interrupted.

Abruptly, Brendan let go of her hand. What gave her the right to demand anything from him? "I'm going to St. Mary's. If you want to come, you can." He started up Dupont Street.

When he glanced back Dai Yue was standing on the sidewalk, her hands clasped tightly in front of her. He gestured for her to follow. She did not shake her head or react in any way; she did not move.

Brendan turned away. He wanted, more than anything, to hold his leather pouch. The money in it had taken him three years to save. Three years of listening to old man Hansen's tirades.

Brendan walked faster. The Chinese girl would be fine. She was less than a mile from her family. And she obviously did not want his help. Brendan refused to look back. She was probably gone by now, taking some other route back to Chinatown. It was rumored that Chinatown was built on top of a warren of underground passages. Maybe she knew some secret way home.

A man wearing six expensive hats, one stacked on top of the other, passed him. Brendan blinked. He knew one of those hats was worth more than everything in his leather pouch. The man was whistling, smiling, as though he were talking a stroll for his health.

Brendan followed him for half a block, entranced by the man's strangeness, the stares that he drew from the crowd.

"Help me with this."

Brendan felt a hand on his arm. The gray-haired woman was wearing a ruffled lavender dressing gown. Her lips were rouged and her hair stuck up in every direction. It looked wet and smelled of perfumed soap.

"Help me. Are you deaf, dearie?"

Brendan shook his head. The woman was like a figure from a dream. The street, the people, even the blue sky above his head and the sun streaming down between the buildings seemed false, like scenery on a stage that could be snatched away at any second.

"Just carry this for me."

The woman was pointing at an iron birdcage. Inside it, a big gray parrot with crimson tail feathers was pacing back and forth on its perch.

"Please hurry up," the woman commanded.

"Hurry up," the parrot echoed.

Brendan blinked. The bird had matched its

mistress's voice exactly. The woman tapped Brendan's shoulder with a sharp forefinger. "I have a sister in Oakland. I want to get down to the ferry at the end of Market Street."

Brendan reached up to tighten the bandage Dai Yue had wrapped around his head. The crowd of oddly dressed people was thickening by the moment. Through the shifting throng he caught a glimpse of Dai Yue. She had not moved from where he'd left her. Brendan shook his head in disbelief.

"You won't? You won't help me?" The woman in lavender ruffles began to cry. The parrot tilted its head to one side, watching her.

"I'll carry the cage back down to Market Street," Brendan said quickly.

The tears vanished and the woman smiled like a happy child. "Fine. Market Street, then. At least it's a start."

Brendan put his arms around the cage and lifted. It was heavy, but he could manage if he walked slowly. The parrot crossed its perch and reached through the bars to fiddle with his shirt buttons. Brendan worked his way along the sidewalk. He stopped twice to get a grip on the cage. The woman waited impatiently each time.

Brendan finally spotted Dai Yue. Her eyes were moving, flickering across the crowds as people passed her. She still had not moved at all and her posture was rigid, tense. As he watched a man bumped into her and shouted angrily. Dai Yue lowered her head as he finished his cursing. Brendan tried to walk faster. The bottom of the birdcage banged his knees painfully with every step. He kept his eyes on Dai Yue. She took two uncertain steps, then stopped again.

Dai Yue was trying hard to calm her breathing. Her head felt too large, full of air; her thoughts spun like kites. The earth was going to shake again. Day Leong was not finished with them yet. She was sure of it. The earth would leap and twist and she would fall beneath the feet of all these ugly Fon Kwei. They would trample her. Or maybe they would turn upon her in an instant and beat her to death the way they had killed her cousin. Dai Yue watched the crowd. The pale faces that surrounded her were blank, or laughing absurdly, or scowling in pointless rage—they were all half mad. She was afraid to move, terrified she would bump one of them, would do something that would cause them all to stop and look at her, to notice that she did not belong here with them.

Dai Yue could feel demons all around her, too, invisible, ferocious. There were no bells here, no incense, no paintings of tigers or dragons to frighten them away. Nothing was right. Nothing would ever be right again. Dai Yue knew she had ruined everything by running from her uncle's shop. He would not forgive her for her disobedience. Her ancestors would not forgive her.

"Dai Yue!"

She heard the boy's voice and felt her heart ease a little. A moment later she saw him, carrying a parrot cage that was nearly as tall as he. A Fon Kwei woman in a loose, flapping dress followed him, her face too pale, too pink.

Dai Yue strengthened herself against false hope. There was no reason to assume this boy would help her. He had been angry when he left.

She watched him as he went by, barely nodding. She had to blink back tears. He carried the birdcage to the corner. She was sure that within a few seconds, he would pass out of sight, and she would be truly alone. But he set the cage down and stood talking to the woman. When he finally started back toward Dai Yue, she began to cry.

"I'm sorry I left you here," the boy said when he got closer.

Dai Yue nodded, wiping at her face, ashamed of her weakness. "I not afraid."

The boy smiled. "Of course not. And my old man never touched a drop of whiskey in his life."

Dai Yue searched his eyes. She had understood most of the words, but couldn't see what his father's drinking habits had to do with anything. His earnest eyes were on hers. Their pale blue color made him look dreamy and strange, like a very old man who could not see far.

Dai Yue hated being this close to so many Fon Kwei. "We go now?"

The boy seemed not to hear her. "There are fires starting up everywhere, I bet."

Dai Yue glanced up at the tall buildings. Most of them were brick. Would they burn? She shuddered, thinking of her uncle's wooden shop, the plank buildings on either side of it that had been built so close that the walls touched.

She looked up the street, wondering which way she should go to find her way home. The buildings were close together. There were business offices on the lower floors, but there were curtains, not signs in the upper stories. People were poking about the doorways like ants after their hill has been kicked apart.

Dai Yue closed her eyes against the whirl of thoughts. She had to get home now, but she had no idea which way the wagon had brought her. How could she have been so foolish? *But,* a voice whispered in her mind, *if you go back, you will have to marry Chou Yee.* She shuddered.

"Are you sick?" The Fon Kwei boy searched her face. His blue eyes looked like glass. "I think we'd better go."

Dai Yue nodded. She tried to move, but her feet would not obey her. The boy took her hand. He pulled, gently, and she found herself able to follow.

"Got yourself a friend?" A tall, leering man leaned toward them as they passed. His back was against a brick wall, a bottle in his right hand. He grinned at Dai Yue's glance. She quickly looked away. Her eyes skipped over a dead cart horse, a weeping woman, a tree split down its center, the white inner wood laid bare.

"I have to get something from St. Mary's," the boy was saying. "You can wait for me, though. I won't be long."

Dai Yue nodded, hoping she had understood. Maybe by the time they got to the Fon Kwei church, she would find her courage and be able to go on alone. The church was on the edge of Chinatown. Everyone knew its square tower, the slender crosses upon it.

"Oh, God, my baby!"

The Fon Kwei boy hesitated at the sound of the desperate voice. Dai Yue turned to look.

"My baby is in there. She's crying!" A heavyset

woman pounded on a closed door, then spun around, scanning the crowd on the sidewalk. No one responded. Perhaps no one had heard. The streets were noisier now, jammed with people intent on their own troubles and destinations. The woman turned back to the door.

"Why doesn't she just go in?" the boy whispered.

Dai Yue looked at the house. Something was wrong with it, but it took a moment for her to figure it out. When she did, she nudged the Fon Kwei boy. "The house . . . " She searched for the words. "Not straight up. Door not open."

The boy looked puzzled, then his eyes lit. "The frame is crooked?"

Dai Yue did not understand the word "crooked," but she nodded, sure he had gotten her meaning. As if to illustrate her thoughts, the woman had taken hold of the door handle and was jerking on it, sobbing, frantic.

The Fon Kwei boy squeezed Dai Yue's hand, then released it and stepped off the sidewalk. "I'll be right back. Stay here."

Dai Yue watched him go, the cold fear seeping

back into her stomach. She did not want to be alone. Making a sudden decision, she followed him across the street.

"My baby is in there!" the woman shouted as they got closer.

"Maybe I can help," the boy called.

Dai Yue watched the woman. Her tear-streaked face was desperate. "Some other men tried. They tried and they couldn't. They said they would come back, but they . . . " Her voice trailed off.

The Fon Kwei boy walked up the steps and tried pulling on the door handle. He braced his feet, then heaved backward. He tried twice more. Giving up, he stepped back, lifting his chin as he looked upward.

Dai Yue followed his gaze up the brick wall. There were three windows on the second story. A business sign with the crawling-bug writing of the Fon Kwei blazoned across it hung beneath the open window that faced the street. Dai Yue watched the boy. She saw him measure the distance to the window with his eyes, then look at her.

"If I stood on that," he said slowly, pointing

at the heap of rubble from the collapsed building next door, "I could climb up, I think." He gestured at the window.

"Maybe fall down," Dai Yue objected. But then she heard the baby crying. She imagined how frightened it must be, how alone. She looked at the pile of debris. The boy was already moving away from her, picking his way through the twisted boards at the foot of the heap.

Dai Yue watched him climb. About halfway up, some of the wreckage slid under his weight. He lifted his arms to catch his balance. The woman had begun to cry again, but it was a muffled sound now, muted with hope. The boy made it to the top of the heap and stood looking at the window.

The Fon Kwei boy stretched up, his fingertips spread out against the side of the building. His hands rested about a foot beneath the windowsill. He repositioned his feet and reached up again. The baby's cries were less shrill now, a thinning wail.

"Oh God, he can't," the mother sobbed. "He can't reach the window." Dai Yue felt the woman's heavy hand on her shoulder. "My baby."

The last two words were so full of sadness that Dai Yue suddenly saw past the woman's flushed pink face and bleary light-colored eyes, all the way to the sorrow in her heart.

Dai Yue started up the pile of rubble. She snagged her trousers on a splintered plank and bent to free herself. When she stood up, she saw the boy looking down at her. "I help," she called to him. He nodded, glancing up at the windowsill.

Dai Yue placed her feet very carefully, pausing several times to look upward. When she was finally on top of the pile, she made her way toward the boy. "Stand here," she told him, patting her own back. She bent over, her palms flat against the brick.

"Are you sure?" the boy asked.

"I am strong," Dai Yue told him. It was true. He would have to trust her.

The boy sat in the rubble and pulled off his boots. He stood and a second later, she felt his foot on her back. It took the boy three tries, but he finally managed to stand, teetering, on her back, long enough to get a grip on the windowsill.

The instant his weight lifted, Dai Yue straightened to watch him scramble through the open window. Then she glanced down at the woman. Her face was impossibly pale, her cheeks were still wet with tears, her hands were wound around each other. Dai Yue looked back at the window and waited.

The noise in the street below swelled, then ebbed. Dai Yue heard little bits of the talk, understood some of it. The mother began to sing quietly, swaying back and forth.

"Dai Yue." The boy's voice made her look up. He had a bundle of blankets in his arms. A little fist jutted up toward his face, grasping.

"My baby!" The woman stood weeping at the edge of the tangle of wood and brick.

"Dai Yue." The boy's voice was an arrow that pierced the street noise, the woman's hysterical crying. He held the baby out, feigning a gentle toss without really letting go. "Can you catch her?"

Dai Yue nodded. It was the best way. It was

probably the only way. The mother was trying to climb now, fighting her awkward Fon Kwei skirts. Soon, she would be close enough to get in the way.

Dai Yue set her feet carefully on the uneven wreckage. She looked up at the boy and spread her arms. "I can."

"Ready?" he asked. He held the baby out.

"Yes," Dai Yue said. The boy leaned out and let the baby go.

The mother screamed and pitched forward, crying out in terror. But the baby dropped straight and true, a gentle fall into Dai Yue's arms. She climbed downward to hand the baby to the mother.

"You could have killed her," the woman spat. Then she held her child close and began to cry again, tears running down her already wet cheeks. "Thank you. Oh, God, thank you."

Dai Yue nodded politely. She glanced back up at the window. The boy had crawled out like a monkey. He hung, looking back over his shoulder. Dai Yue moved to give him room. Once she was clear he jumped, rolling sideways when he hit the rubble, falling hard enough to lose his breath for a few seconds.

Dai Yue waited until he got to his feet and handed him his boots. She struggled to remember the correct words. "Tell me your name," she said carefully. "Again."

The Fon Kwei boy grinned at her, brushing splinters and brick dust off his trousers. "Brendan. Brendan O'Connor."

CHAPTER FIVE

Brendan scrambled down. The baby had stopped crying, comforted instantly by her mother's voice.

"I can't thank you enough," the mother was saying as he stepped out of the shattered wood and fallen brick. Brendan nodded politely. He glanced southward. There were spires of smoke that looked like they were coming from the Mission District. Maybe the bakery would burn down.

"You hurt?"

Dai Yue's voice was quiet and close. Brendan looked at her. "No. You were right. You are strong."

A shy smile fluttered at the corners of Dai

Yue's lips, then disappeared. Her eyes darted over the crowds in the street. Brendan followed her gaze. A Japanese man was struggling to carry a gilt-framed painting through the crowded street.

"Look at that," the baby's mother said from behind Brendan. "A portrait of their Emperor. Why would he take that?"

Brendan shook his head. "My mother would have taken her statue of Jesus."

The woman smiled wryly. "I won't have to decide. I can't get back in to take anything." She patted her baby's back, looking down into the little face. "The most important thing to me is right here."

"We had better be going now," Brendan said, glancing at Dai Yue. She nodded, then her hands flew up to cover her mouth. Brendan felt the earth shift beneath them.

The ground quivered, an odd rolling sensation. Brendan stood, clenching both fists, every muscle in his body tense. The mother began to weep. Dai Yue stood like an ivory statue. The crowds stilled and for a second, the city echoed in another strange, deep silence broken only by the church bells. Then the tremor ended and people came back to life.

"May? Oh, God, May!"

Brendan saw a man shoving toward them. He was tall, wearing the rough clothes of a laborer. He leapt up the stairs and encircled the woman in his arms, then leaned back to peer at the baby.

"Is she all right?"

"These two got her out through the upper window." The woman gestured at Dai Yue and Brendan. "I couldn't open the door." She pushed her hair back out of her eyes. "Thomas, the door is ruined. We can't get back in."

"Thank you for your help," the man said. "May God watch over you both." He picked up a long board and faced the door of his apartment. He began to beat at the unyielding wood.

Brendan led Dai Yue back into the milling throngs that filled the sidewalk and spilled over into the street. It seemed impossible that so many people lived in San Francisco. Even on the busiest day on Market Street he had never seen crowds like this. People were shoving and shouting at each other. They were praying and weeping and laughing at nothing. No one seemed to know which direction to go.

"Make way, make way!"

The gruff voice startled Brendan. Dai Yue stepped aside, with Brendan close behind her. Two workmen labored along the sidewalk, pushing an enormous piano made of glistening dark wood. A little girl stumbled in front of the piano, but her mother lifted her in time, running a few steps to get out of the way.

Brendan held tightly to Dai Yue's hand and started walking. He could tell she was close to panic again. The crowds seemed to terrify her.

The piano movers slowed as Dupont Street began to rise. Brendan looked up the hill. It only got steeper. The two men paused to rest, leaning against the piano to keep it from rolling. People streamed around them. As Brendan and Dai Yue passed they could hear the men arguing in low voices about whether they could possibly make it all the way to Nob Hill.

Brendan glanced back over his shoulder. Smoke was rising steadily from three or four places south of The Slot now. It was black smoke, roiling in spires that blurred and joined as they drifted higher above Market Street. Brendan heard the distant clanging of a fire bell. He felt the stir of a breeze against his face. If the wind came up, the firemen would have a harder time putting out the fires.

Brendan felt Dai Yue tug at his hand. She pointed, a questioning look on her face. Brendan followed her gesture. The hill rose gently, then more sharply closer to Chinatown. Near the top, soldiers were marching onto Dupont Street.

"Soldiers," Brendan said wonderingly.

Dai Yue looked puzzled. She seemed to be searching for a word. "War?" she asked hesitantly.

Brendan shook his head, his eyes fixed on the men marching down the street toward them. There were fifteen or twenty of them. The man at the head of the column was shouting to people as they passed. When he got closer, Brendan could make out most of what he was saying.

" . . . looters will be shot. No junk thieves will be tolerated. This is General Funston's order and all troops will carry it out. Spread the word."

"What's looting?" Brendan asked a man just in front of him.

"Going through the ruined shops. Stealing."

Brendan nodded, then turned to Dai Yue. Her hand had tightened on his. "The soldiers will shoot thieves. That's all. No war."

Dai Yue looked relieved, but her grip on his hand didn't relax. The crowd carried them along like a river's current. The sidewalk slanted in places, and there were cracks in it from the earthquake. Here and there water gushed down the gutter. Water pipes had broken. Brendan saw people stare at him and Dai Yue, their eyes sliding away when he looked at them.

Brendan heard an odd whistling sound. He turned and suddenly noticed a crop of spiky gray hair, still uncombed and sticky with soap. It was the parrot woman, walking along not far behind them. He slowed, working his way back through a group of men, tugging Dai Yue with him. The woman had found a child's wagon somewhere. She was pulling the birdcage in it. The parrot was cleaning its feathers.

"Hello again, young man," the woman said when she saw him. Her face lit with a smile. "I didn't get much farther than Market Street. They've closed the ferries. There's no way to get in or out of San Francisco."

Brendan nodded. Walking along beside the wagon, he put a finger through the cage bars. The parrot reached to nibble it gently with its great black beak.

"I suppose there's no place like home," the woman joked. She was breathing hard. "Especially when you can't seem to go anywhere else."

The parrot tilted its head to get a better look at Brendan. Dai Yue touched it through the bars. It ruffled its feathers and ducked its head.

"He wants you to scratch his cheek," the woman said. "Caruso rarely takes to strangers and I always trust his opinions."

Brendan watched Dai Yue rub Caruso's cheek with the tip of her index finger.

"He sang this morning," the woman said. "At least that's what people are saying."

Brendan looked up, trying not to laugh. "He sings?"

"Of course Caruso sings. He is the most famous opera performer in the world. I named the parrot after him."

Brendan shot a look at Dai Yue. She was still rubbing the parrot's cheek. Was she understanding any of this?

The gray-haired woman stopped, pressing one hand into the small of her back. "Caruso stayed at the Palace last night," she said. "This morning after the earthquake, they say he sang from an open window. I would give anything to have heard him." The woman's face was radiant, her eyes shining. For a moment she looked like a little girl.

"I help you?" Dai Yue said to the woman. She reached out and took the wagon handle. The woman relinquished it, smiling. She took a hankie from her bodice and dabbed at her forehead. "I am most grateful. My name is Miss Agatha Toland."

Brendan introduced himself and Dai Yue shyly said her own name.

Miss Toland gestured up the hill and they started walking. "Where are you two going?"

Brendan hesitated. He did not want to explain to anyone why he had to get St. Mary's.

"I go home," Dai Yue said.

Brendan nodded. "I'm taking her back to Chinatown."

"You are a kind soul, Brendan." Miss Toland ran her fingers through her spiky hair. It had dried, a white film of soap framing her forehead. No one seemed to notice—many people were half dressed or still in their nightclothes.

As they crossed Post Street, Brendan helped Dai Yue ease the wagon from the sidewalk onto the cobblestones, then back up on the other side. Miss Toland pointed. "Look at that. So many are heading toward Union Square. I wonder if all their homes were destroyed."

Brendan shrugged. If his cot and blanket had burned up along with the rest of the warehouse, he would have to find another place to sleep.

Miss Toland stopped again, breathing hard. "It's a terrible thing, really. It's as if God is punishing this city. It seems we no sooner rebuild from a fire or an earthquake than we have to start all over again. The quake of '90 ruined my uncle. He lost everything. Poor man never recovered."

Brendan cast a sidelong glance at Miss Toland as she led the way again. He dropped back to walk behind the wagon, pushing to help Dai Yue get it up the hill. The parrot came to his side of the cage and made soft cooing sounds. Half a block farther, they stopped again to rest. Brendan looked back down toward Market Street. The columns of smoke were swelling. Why weren't the firemen putting out the fires?

Miss Toland was bending over the birdcage. The big gray parrot put his face close to hers. "I want grapes," he said, very distinctly. "Or apples."

Brendan shook his head. Miss Toland laughed. "It's quite astonishing, isn't it? The odd thing is that he means it. Caruso loves grapes.

And apples. Well," she said, smiling. "Everyone ready?" Without another word, Miss Toland strode uphill again.

As they got close to St. Mary's, Brendan tried frantically to figure out what he was going to do. Miss Toland kept talking and he nodded to be polite, but he wasn't really listening. Dai Yue walked at a steady pace, her posture tense, her eyes always returning to the smoke hanging over the Mission District.

California Street was teeming with people leaving Chinatown. They all carried baskets and bundles of their belongings. Some of them pushed handcarts. Dai Yue maneuvered the wagon through to the sidewalk, scanning the faces as people passed. It took Brendan a moment to understand that she was probably looking for her uncle.

Brendan smiled when he saw the bell tower of St. Mary's still standing. The inscription beneath the clock face stood out in high relief in the slanting morning sunlight. "Son, observe the time and fly from evil." Brendan glanced down the long sidewall. The bricks were all still intact. So his pouch was safe. He made a sudden decision to leave it where it was. If he took it out now, a hundred people would wonder what was so valuable. Even if no one robbed him, he could never use the hiding place again.

"Well, I'll be turning here." Miss Toland took the wagon handle from Dai Yue. "You are two lovely children. Keep yourselves safe."

Brendan watched as Miss Toland pulled the wagon on down California Street, her lavender gown flapping in the breeze.

"Good Fon Kwei lady," Dai Yue murmured.

"What?" Brendan looked at Dai Yue, then shrugged his shoulders when she didn't answer. He pointed to St. Mary's. "I have to go in there. Wait for me here. I won't be long."

Without waiting for an answer, Brendan walked away from her. He pushed open the heavy wooden door. At the font, he dipped his fingers and crossed himself. Inside, the church was crowded. People prayed in hushed voices. Some were kneeling at the marble altar. Others sat in the pews, their rosary beads clicking through their fingers.

Brendan crossed himself and approached the altar. He knelt and prayed to St. Jude. Standing, he crossed himself again. For a few seconds, he hesitated, considering lighting candles for his parents. His mother had been devout. His father, if he were alive, would be working on a drunk right now. The idea of candles would make him laugh.

Brendan made his way back down the aisle. The stained glass window splintered the sunlight into a hundred colors. The murals on the walls seemed vivid, like living scenes beneath the high ceiling. The very walls seemed to breathe hope, calmness. Brendan wet his fingertips in the holy water, then hesitated again. He hated to leave. He didn't want to see the frightened faces in the streets, the smoke that was beginning to cloak the city. He took a deep breath and pushed on the door, then went out. He had taken three steps when the earth jolted beneath his feet again.

CHAPTER SIX

Dai Yue screamed before she could stop herself. The tremor moved through the earth, into her belly, rattling the calmness that she had worked so hard to maintain. The Earth Dragon Day Leong was still angry, still shifting. The Fon Kwei going in and out of the church had all noticed her, their curiosity plain to see. She had wanted to shout at them, to tell them she had no interest in their temple, their weak Fon Kwei god.

Now, as the earth trembled, she wondered if their god could hear her thoughts so close to his temple. Had she angered him? Was this a warning? Or was this the tremor that would open the earth at her feet and swallow her? She closed her eyes and tried not to imagine the weight of earth and fallen bricks crushing her.

"Dai Yue!"

She looked up to see Brendan running toward her, his steps labored, off-balance, as he fought the shaking in the ground. He ran, taking a serpent's path through the frightened people who stood in ragged groups on the sidewalk. One woman was still wailing, her voice high-pitched, almost painful to hear. An older man sank to the ground and sat, his eyes empty as a bewildered child's. Brendan reached Dai Yue and clasped her hand.

She looked into his strange Fon Kwei face. The earth beneath their feet heaved once more, then lay still again. Brendan shook his head. "I will sure be glad when that stops happening."

Dai Yue nodded. She turned, still holding his hand, and began walking up Dupont Gai. All she could think about now was her uncle. Was he alive? And would he speak to her or turn her aside for her disobedience?

Dai Yue blinked. Her eyes stung from the smoke in the air. As they went, the tide of humanity coming toward them increased. There were more and more Celestials here—her own people. Handcarts clattered over the cobblestones, shouts and arguments rang out as wagons and pedestrians competed for room in the street. Dai Yue saw three little boys, still small enough to be dressed by their cautious mother like little girls. Boys were important. They attracted demons more often than girls. Dai Yue shook her head. Maybe girls' clothing would fool the demons, but Day Leong could surely see through the ruse.

Dai Yue heard fragments of conversation as they wove their way along. Everyone was talking about the same thing—there were fires in Chinatown. There were fires all around it. People were afraid.

As they approached the Street of the Sons of Tang, Dai Yue saw a mass of people moving uneasily along the sidewalk in front of the boot and shoe factory. There was a solid line of workers all the way across the front of the tea store. Of course, she realized. None of the factory workers would want to stay at their benches, but they would be reluctant to leave without permission. Any man who went home without permission risked losing his job.

Dai Yue walked faster. Some of the saloons had women standing in front of them, shawls wrapped hastily over their gaudy dresses. The tailor shop was damaged. Its front windows had shattered, spraying a glitter of glass out into the street. A strong, warm odor of tobacco drifted from the cigar factories.

"How much farther?" Brendan asked.

Dai Yue gestured. "Not far." She searched his eyes. Was he going to leave her here? She glanced around. Among the hundreds of men were a few women. Some of them looked respectable. Perhaps she could ask one of them for news of her uncle, for help.

A man bumped into Dai Yue and Brendan tightened his hold on her hand. "Show me which way you need to go." He leaned close and almost shouted so that she could hear him over the street noise.

Dai Yue nodded, then noticed a man staring at her. She averted her eyes, only to meet the gaze of another man glaring in her direction. She became acutely aware of Brendan's hand on hers. What would her uncle think when he saw them walking together? What would he do?

There were only a few people headed toward the center of Chinatown. The street was swarming with dark-coated men trying to get out. Here and there women and children walked with their heads down, their possessions tied in bundles on their backs.

Dai Yue walked beside Brendan along Sacramento Street. She was grateful for his kindness, but the closer they got to Chinatown's narrow streets, the more foolish she felt. Her uncle was not going to welcome this stranger.

Dai Yue tried to hurry. For the first time she realized that her feet hurt. She was not used to walking so far on cobblestones. She turned left onto Brooklyn Place, cutting in front of two old men as she passed the laundry on the corner. She waited until they were past the shirt factory, then looked back. Some of the lodgers on the second story of the laundry were on their balconies, gathering up their belongings.

Dai Yue darted into an alleyway, Brendan close behind her. She saw a collapsed lodging house and caught a glimpse of someone trapped in the wreckage. She turned right, then left, passing a restaurant and a tailor's shop. On the next block, four buildings lay in ruins. Dai Yue could feel her heart thudding against her ribs. Two more turns, and she would be able to see her uncle's pharmacy. She was so frightened and so worried that several seconds passed before she realized that the earth was moving once more.

The ground beneath her feet quivered, then jolted. The street noise died for a few seconds, then rose again. Dai Yue felt her heart quicken with fear, but the tremor was over so quickly that she didn't have time to get really frightened. Still, the tremor seemed to shake her free of her indecision. She stopped and faced Brendan. "You go now. I am home."

He looked puzzled. "Where? Here? You live in one of the shop buildings?"

She shook her head. "You go. I thank you."

Brendan was looking into her eyes. "Are you sure?"

Dai Yue nodded, freeing her hand from his. "Yes."

Brendan's eyes clouded and she saw that he was afraid of something. She looked around the crowded street. Was it as strange for him to be surrounded by her people as it was for her to be surrounded by his?

"You go home," Dai Yue said gently.

Brendan hesitated. "I stay in a warehouse down by the ferry." He shrugged. "From the hill it looked like that whole stretch was on fire."

"You have no father?"

Brendan shook his head. "And it's better that way. I do all right."

"I have only uncle," Dai Yue said. She searched for a Fon Kwei word to describe her uncle's strict, cold nature. "He is mean."

She watched Brendan's eyes cloud again. "My father was mean when he was drunk."

"Uncle not drink." Dai Yue hesitated. His eyes remained on hers, questioning. "He find husband." She stopped again, her eyes flooding, unable to say more.

"For you? Someone you don't like?"

Dai Yue wiped at her eyes. "An old man. Fat. Mean."

Brendan kicked at the cobblestones. "He can't make you marry someone like that."

Dai Yue nodded. "Chou Yee have good family. Rich."

Brendan was shaking his head. "But if you don't like him—"

"I go now. I thank you."

Before Brendan could answer, Dai Yue turned and ran. She rounded the corner, then turned once more, racing down the narrow alley. She burst out onto the street and stumbled to a halt, looking wildly down the block. There were four men lighting strips of scarlet paper afire and tossing them down into a hole they had dug. Dai Yue hoped their offerings of sacred red paper would appease Day Leong, calm him.

Dai Yue started up the street, disoriented, then realized her uncle's shop was a pile of rubble.

The three buildings between it and the corner had fallen too. A brick lodging house still stood on this side of the street, but little else.

Dai Yue began to run again, her breath quick little explosions of worry. She stopped in front of the mountain of fractured planks and twisted pieces of wood that had been her uncle's store a few hours before. Scattered through the wreckage, she saw, were broken jars and bottles, their precious contents lost.

"Uncle?"

Dai Yue listened. There was no answer.

"Uncle?" Dai Yue called a second time. A scrap of dark blue cloth caught her eye. She ducked under a protruding beam, then began to climb through the wreckage, her eyes fastened on the cloth. She knew it was her uncle before she could actually see him. When she did, she caught her breath, scared that he was dead.

"Uncle!"

He moved slightly, groaning. Dai Yue tried to shift the planks that lay uppermost on the pile of wreckage that had pinned her uncle down.

"Uncle!" she screamed.

He opened his eyes. "Dai Yue," he said, and closed them once more. The ground began to vibrate. Bricks fell, slamming against broken boards a few feet from Dai Yue. She crouched, covering her head with her arms.

CHAPTER SEVEN

Brendan stood, his heart slamming in his chest as the earth quivered and rolled. The wind bells hanging from the balconies above his head swayed, ringing. A shower of bricks crashed around him and he flinched. For a second he tried to make himself run. But what good would that do? Any building could be the one to collapse, to bury him alive.

Finally, the shaking stopped. Brendan was tired, he was hungry, and he felt more alone than he had since the day his father died. He heard shouts and looked up. A heavy-jowled woman stood on a second-story balcony. She was yelling at him, the words razor-sharp and coldly unfamiliar.

Without thinking, Brendan ran until her voice faded behind him. Then he stopped again. He shivered. His old bakery route had included two stops at the white groceries on Dupont Street in the middle of Chinatown. Usually, he liked the exotic smells and sounds, the sight of the black-coated men with their long queues and the delicate, flowerlike women. But the alleys and the narrow streets had always scared him.

All his life, people had told him there were tunnels beneath the streets, miles of them, where the opium addicts and the lepers lived. Brendan had never talked to anyone who had actually seen the tunnels, but it seemed possible. There was an air of secrets and mystery in Chinatown.

Four men appeared around the corner. Their faces were twisted into grim frowns. They walked fast, one older man in front of the others. Brendan tried to step aside, but he wasn't fast enough. The older man pushed past him. One of the three who followed pushed him a second time, glaring into his face.

Brendan regained his balance. When none of them even looked back at him, his heart began to slow. He waited until they were almost out of sight, then followed the alleyway. He tried to recall the turns Dai Yue had made. It was confusing. The buildings were close together and the signs and bright red banners meant nothing to him.

Turning right, Brendan searched for something familiar about the buildings that would let him know that he was on the right path. Finally he spotted a laundry he was nearly certain they had passed on the way in. A few hundred feet farther on, he bore left into another narrow alleyway.

With every step, Brendan's uneasiness increased. The alleyways were full of people and every time his eyes met someone else's he saw surprise harden into hostility. He wanted to explain why he had come into their part of the city, but he knew he couldn't. So he hurried, glancing up just often enough to keep from bumping into anyone.

As he got closer to Brooklyn Place, Brendan

hesitated. He was starting to regret his decision not to get his pouch. The idea of losing his mother's ring and his father's watch made him feel almost sick.

Shaking his head, Brendan turned right off Brooklyn Place onto Sacramento Street. He hurried past the cigar factories. The lodgers who lived upstairs were scurrying out the front doors, carrying baskets and bundles tied with stiff hemp twine. The crowds were just as thick, but the street was wider, and Brendan's uneasiness lifted a little as he passed the Chinese broom factory, the merchandise stores, and the two white groceries he had delivered to last year. The harsh sound of the conversations around him still grated at his nerves. It was so strange to hear people speak and not to be able to understand anything they were saying.

At the corner Brendan turned right and started down Dupont. He thought about crossing, but the acrid smell of the meat market unsettled his already queasy stomach. He hurried past the Japanese and Chinese Bazaar. The solid line of workers in front of the boot and shoe factory was beginning to thin out. The tea store had closed, its door boarded shut.

Brendan walked with his head down, his hands in his pockets. He saw some of the Chinese men looking at him sidelong, but they were all too preoccupied to do more than notice him. The air was hazy with smoke now and it was impossible to see far enough to tell where it was coming from.

St. Mary's was still surrounded by people as Brendan got closer. He could see dozens of women kneeling near the doors, praying. He turned on California Street and edged along the sidewalk.

A woman in a huge Gainsborough hat was arguing with a policeman. The false grapes and cherries that decorated her hat bobbed in time with her wide gestures. Brendan couldn't hear what she was saying, but it was obvious that the policeman was trying to detach himself, to walk away. The woman clung to his arm, her voice earnest. As Brendan watched, the officer lifted her hand and tried to leave.

"Is that you, Brendan O'Connor?" someone shouted.

Brendan recognized Mr. Malloy's deep voice. The tall man was heading toward him. As he got closer, Brendan saw the heavy gray shadows under his eyes. One of his cheeks was smudged with black and his usually perfect suit coat was torn.

Malloy called out again when he was halfway across the street. "What are you still doing here, son? Get the girl home all right?

Brendan waited until Malloy was beside him to answer. "I think so. She told me to leave, then ran off."

Malloy nodded. "I'm glad you got out of there. The fires are sweeping that way, and fast. The whole Financial District is burning and so is half the town south of The Slot."

Brendan automatically turned to face Market Street, even though the haze of smoke made it impossible to see more than half a block away. "Are the firemen putting it out?"

Malloy laughed, a blunt, angry sound. "There's no water. The main on Seventh and

Howard is broken. So are others, I am told. The reservoir pipes have been sheared off. They are using the old downtown cisterns now, but there aren't that many of them left and no one seems quite sure where most of them are."

Brendan blinked. "No water?" He was suddenly aware of his thirst. He wiped the back of his hand across his mouth. "How is anyone going to drink? I mean . . . "

"Here," Mr. Malloy said. He pulled a silver flask from inside his jacket.

Brendan shook his head emphatically. "Thank you, sir. But my father drank and I swore I'd never touch—"

"I wouldn't offer a boy your age whiskey," Malloy assured him. "This is water. I filled it from the Howard Street geyser where the main broke. Figured I'd need it before the day was out."

Brendan took the flask gratefully. The water tasted sweeter than any he had ever drunk. He wanted to gulp down all of it, but he took two swallows, then handed the flask back.

Malloy pocketed the flask, then pulled a

small clipboard out of his pocket, along with a stubbed pencil. "So tell me what you've seen. You were up in Chinatown?"

"Yes, sir."

"How does it look?"

Brendan hesitated, unsure what to say. "It looks pretty bad. Most of the buildings are damaged and quite a few are collapsed. The people are scared. Most of them are leaving, carrying whatever they can. There are a lot of families. You usually don't see the women or children."

Malloy tapped his pencil, looking up. "You might have a future in reporting if you want one. That's the kind of thing most people miss."

Brendan managed a smile. "I'd like to be a reporter, sir."

Malloy smiled back. "It'll take years off your life, but it's damned exciting."

A distant thudding boom made Brendan stiffen, but there was no tremor in the ground. People all around them stopped for an instant, then went on.

Mr. Malloy looked at his watch before making

a note on the smudged paper on his clipboard. "That's dynamite," he said, looking up.

"Dynamite?" Brendan echoed. "I thought it was just gas mains exploding or drugstore chemicals."

Malloy was still making notes. "We've had that, too. But this is the army. They're trying to make firebreaks, a wide enough space so that the flames can't jump over. They thought Market Street would be wide enough, but it wasn't."

Brendan heard someone shouting orders. He turned to look. Soldiers brandishing rifles were going door-to-door. Brendan glanced at Mr. Malloy.

"They're evacuating people. It's past time you got out of here. Chinatown is going to be an inferno in the next few hours. Even sooner if the evening breeze rises."

Brendan glanced back up Dupont Street. Dai Yue and her uncle were probably already walking along some sidewalk together, carrying as many of their belongings as they could manage. He envied her fiercely for a second. Maybe her uncle was harsh, but he cared about her, about the kind of life she was going to live.

"Are you listening, son? I told you it's time to get out of this part of the city. The soldiers are setting up refugee camps in the parks and squares. Brendan?"

Brendan focused on Mr. Malloy. "I heard you," he said. "Thanks."

Mr. Malloy gripped Brendan's shoulder. "When all this is over, you come see me. The Call Building is on fire, so you'll have to find out where we've moved the offices. But if there's a job, I'll see to it that you get it. You take care now." Without another word, Mr. Malloy walked away, heading up California Street toward Nob Hill.

Brendan watched him go. There was another dull booming sound, but this time the earth rose and fell beneath Brendan's feet. He heard one woman gasp, but everyone else simply paused, like children when the music stops in a parlor game.

Brendan stood still. A half dozen soldiers were gathered in a little knot, and a man was standing before them with his hands in the air. His shirt was tattered and streaked with grime. One of the soldiers backed away, leveling his rifle at the man's stomach.

Without warning, the man bolted and ran into the crowd, shoving people aside. The soldier took aim and held his rifle to his shoulder, but did not fire. It was impossible to shoot into the mass of people that clogged the street, fleeing in front of the flames.

People rushed past Brendan, walking in family groups, in couples, holding each other. He headed up California Street, but then stopped. He turned and looked at the rising wall of smoke. Here and there he saw sparkles within it. Flames? He turned around and started running back toward Chinatown.

CHAPTER EIGHT

Dai Yue's fear was like a live thing inside of her. She pressed her hands against her stomach to trap it there, to keep it from racing through her body. She could still hear her uncle's mumbled pleas, yet she was helpless to do anything. She had dragged away splintered boards and shards of glass, but her digging had done no good. Her uncle was still buried, and even worse, he seemed weaker now.

"Uncle?" she said softly, reaching through the tangle of wreckage to take his bloodied hand. She held it, wondering what she should do, what she could do. This time she heard the wind chimes before she felt the trembling in the ground.

Accompanied by the clear, discordant brass chimes, the earth rose and fell. Then it seemed to shake itself once more before it quieted. Dai Yue held tightly to her uncle's hand, even once the ground was still again. Dull explosions, the same ones she had been hearing for an hour or more, followed the tremor. Dai Yue didn't know what they were, but the sounds frightened her—they were getting closer.

She squeezed her uncle's hand. He didn't respond. There was a light touch on her cheek and she looked up, startled. She blinked. Ashes, carried on the breeze, swirled above her like miscolored snow.

Dai Yue's uncle pushed futilely against the heavy timbers that had trapped him. He shoved, sweat springing out on his face. Then he fell back, his face pale. "Dai Yue. Get me out. The fire is close."

"I cannot, Uncle." She felt her tears, warm and wet on her cheeks.

"You must." Each word was spoken slowly and carefully.

"If I had not run away this morning—"

"Foolish child. Just get help."

"I will try. But it will be difficult. Everyone is running."

"Find Chou Yee. He will help."

"But Uncle—"

"Go now."

Dai Yue tried to find her voice. She knew she should honor her uncle's wish.

"Hey! Dai Yue? Come on, you have to get out of here!"

Dai Yue straightened at the sound of Brendan's sudden shout. He was running toward her, one arm in front of his face to protect his eyes from the floating ash.

"Come on. The fires are closing in."

Dai Yue whispered Brendan's name, afraid to believe that he was real.

"Dai Yue? Are you hurt?"

She shook her head, then finally managed to answer. "My uncle . . . " She pointed, and Brendan came to stand beside her.

"Oh, my God!" Brendan knelt. He touched first one timber, then another.

Dai Yue heard her uncle's curse and she

bent closer, explaining quickly that Brendan had helped her get home. Her uncle glared at her, struggling feebly against the weight of the rubble.

Brendan faced her. "Tell him to stop moving."

Dai Yue watched as Brendan prowled along the edges of the wreckage that had been her uncle's pharmacy. He moved stiffly, in quick, nervous jerks that told her how frightened he was. But when he spoke, his voice was clear and steady.

"Help me with this."

Dai Yue ran to grasp the long, stout board. Alongside Brendan, she strained every muscle, and finally it began to come loose. A moment later, they stood panting side by side, the long board freed, lying at their feet.

"Hurry," Brendan rasped. Dai Yue helped Brendan carry the board, then watched as he pushed it under the beam that had pinned her uncle's legs. Then he carried a wrecked cabinet over and jammed it beneath the long board.

"Help me again," Brendan said.

Following his gestures, Dai Yue leaned her full weight on the long board as Brendan shoved it downward. The beam on her uncle's legs lifted, scraping against the boards that lay around it.

Dai Yue heard her uncle's gasp, then another scraping sound and a sharp intake of breath.

"Is he free?" Brendan asked, the words squeezed out from between his clenched teeth. His face was red with effort.

Dai Yue leaned, trying to see without taking her weight from the board. Her uncle had pulled his legs to one side, his knees bent. "Yes," Dai Yue told Brendan. Together they let the board rise, then fought to get their breath, coughing on the stinging smoke.

Dai Yue's lungs burned painfully as Brendan slid the long board beneath the timber across her uncle's chest. Dai Yue heard her uncle curse and was glad that Brendan could not understand. For her uncle, a Fon Kwei face was a reminder that his only son was dead. He could not know what she had learned—this boy was different.

"Dai Yue!" Brendan was already shoving down on the lever. Dai Yue hurried to help him. This time, as the timber lifted, a series of dull thumping blasts sounded and some of the buildings across the street slumped.

"Tell him we have to hurry," Brendan said as he jerked the long board out of her uncle's way.

Dai Yue helped her uncle, pushing back a tangle of small debris. He was weak, but managed to stand up.

"Ask him if he can walk," Brendan prompted Dai Yue.

She asked, her stomach tightening.

"I can walk," her uncle said.

Dai Yue translated this answer for Brendan as her uncle took a tentative step. At first, he seemed steady, but then he lurched to one side. Dai Yue cried out and leapt to steady him. Without warning, Brendan stepped forward. He ducked beneath her uncle's arm, then straightened up slowly.

Dai Yue saw her uncle's eyes widen. He jerked back and lost his balance again. His legs buckling, he put nearly all of his weight on

Brendan, cursing all Fon Kwei in a low, growling voice.

"What's he saying?" Brendan asked once they had her uncle upright again.

"He thanks you," Dai Yue said.

Brendan started forward. "Keep in step with me," he shouted at her.

Dai Yue kept her eyes on Brendan for the first four or five steps. Then she looked forward again. Together they started down the street.

Dai Yue's uncle walked slowly, and she was afraid he was more hurt than he had admitted. At the corner, he turned to face Dai Yue.

"That way." He jutted his chin to indicate a narrow alley that ran between two buildings.

Dai Yue told Brendan what her uncle had said, and they broke into single file to go down the passageway. At the far end, Dai Yue emerged into a tree-lined garden she had never seen before. Her uncle started across it, walking unevenly. Halfway to the other side, he stumbled. Brendan caught him. Dai Yue's uncle shrugged him off, staggering on alone.

"This way now," Dai Yue's uncle rasped, leading

them through a doorway. They passed down a hallway lined with doors on either side. The hall ran from the back of the house to the front. They came out into a narrow street.

They followed it for a long way, then turned to pass through a tailor's shop, going in the back door and out the front again. They came into another narrow street. Dai Yue's uncle led them across it, slowing to step carefully over a scatter of boards. On the far side, he stopped and bent double, breathing hard.

Dai Yue watched her uncle, worried. The smoke was so thick it was hard to breathe. Her eyes stung and her throat felt raw. She followed her uncle. Brendan kept up, but every few moments he looked back toward the curtain of smoke.

"This way," Dai Yue's uncle commanded.

Dai Yue gestured and Brendan followed them into a meat shop. The smell was overpowering and Dai Yue felt her stomach clench. She realized how hungry she was and longed for a cup of tea to soothe her throat. Her uncle stopped near the front of the shop. There was a bucket sitting on the counter, with a dipper hanging from the rim. Dai Yue stopped, her dry throat aching at the sight of water. "Uncle, I am thirsty," she said.

He leaned on a table, waiting while she drank, then frowned when Brendan took the dipper from her. Dai Yue shot her uncle a glance, knowing that he would refuse to drink after the Fon Kwei boy. When her uncle spat on the floor, Brendan glanced at him, but did not speak.

"Your uncle should drink, too," Brendan said as they started out of the shop. "Mr. Malloy from the newspaper said that all the pipes in the city are broken. That's why they can't fight the fires. Who knows when we will get water again."

Dai Yue translated as much as she had understood. Her uncle only spat once more and hobbled ahead of them, going through the front door and down a few wide steps to the street.

"This is Clay Street," Brendan said quietly as they descended. "This was on my route, too."

He looked surprised to be in familiar territory.

Dai Yue understood only part of what he had said. In the distance, she heard a rapid sequence of muffled blasts. It sounded like a New Year's celebration. Her uncle stopped, a contorted scowl on his face.

"Dai Yue, tell him to go now," her uncle ordered, coughing, jabbing a finger in Brendan's direction. "He will only bring us bad luck."

Dai Yue turned so that Brendan would not see the emotion in her face. "He saved your life, Uncle. You owe him a favor."

"It is already repaid. He could not have found his own way out of the City of the Sons of Tang."

"But he could have left me to die on the Fon Kwei street this morning." Dai Yue was trembling. She had never spoken to her uncle this way.

"I told you," he said in a low voice. "This favor has already been repaid."

Dai Yue was angrier than she had ever been in her life. How could he ignore what Brendan had done? "He saved your life, as well, Uncle. I could not have done it alone. All the others just walked past."

Dai Yue fully expected her uncle to explode into a rage, but he did not. Instead he closed his eyes and took three long breaths. When he did speak, his voice was tight and clipped.

"Tell him I owe him one favor."

Dai Yue translated, accurately this time. Brendan nodded politely, listening to her while watching her uncle's face.

"Explain to him that he doesn't owe me anything," Brendan said.

"He accepts," she said to her uncle, feeling a small twinge at the lie. Lies attracted demons.

"Only one," her uncle responded.

She turned to Brendan. "He owes one favor."

"Then tell him I want you to be able to marry whoever you want," Brendan said. He smiled impishly at her.

Dai Yue caught her breath. She gathered her courage and repeated the favor in Chinese.

Her uncle went rigid, his face draining of color again. He coughed hard for a long time. Dai Yue saw a tiny trickle of blood at the corner of his mouth. "You asked for this favor," her uncle accused once he had caught his breath.

Dai Yue looked into his eyes. "I would not steal what he earned."

Her uncle coughed again. The smoke was getting thicker. "I grant this favor. Now tell him to go."

Dai Yue turned to Brendan. "He says yes. He says you go now."

The startled look on Brendan's face tugged at Dai Yue's heart. She turned to her uncle. "Let him come with us."

Dai Yue's uncle spat once more. "I have no strength to waste in argument." He walked off with an odd swaying motion, then stopped at the corner to cough again. Dai Yue stayed just behind him. When he was not looking, she reached to touch Brendan's hand.

Brendan could barely breathe. The smoke clawed at his throat and lungs as he followed Dai Yue and her uncle along Clay Street. There were so many people fleeing the fires that it was almost impossible to tell which way they should go. There was smoke in every direction. All they could do was keep going, keep heading into areas that weren't yet ablaze.

Dai Yue's uncle was coughing almost constantly now and he leaned heavily on her as they walked. Once or twice Brendan steadied him from the opposite side, but met a glare of such hatred that he backed away again.

Brendan glanced at Dai Yue. She was watching her uncle, her worry showing plainly in her eyes. There was blood on his lips and on his cheeks. He coughed again, doubling over, but somehow he kept going.

The sky was filling with smoke. The street seemed dusky, as though it were evening, not mid-afternoon. There was a strange reddish color in the light, too. It tinted the buildings, people's faces, the ground itself—making everything seem flushed, unnatural.

Brendan felt his stomach grinding. He was so hungry. He had been a fool not to eat at the shops they had walked through. He swallowed painfully. Even more than he wanted food, he wanted water. Brendan felt Dai Yue tug at the back of his shirt. He turned to face her.

"Uncle rest now."

Brendan shook his head. "Not here. The fires are too close."

Dai Yue spoke to her uncle. He spat, cursing, and glared at Brendan. Then he said something to Dai Yue, coughing violently between rushes of angry-sounding words.

"He can go no more," Dai Yue said. "We stop now."

Brendan looked up at the sky. The smoke had closed over the city now, shutting out the sun, cutting San Francisco off from the rest of the world. Brendan felt the tug on his shirt again.

"We stop there." Dai Yue pointed at the corner.

"Only for a few minutes," Brendan told her. He could see that her uncle was badly hurt, but if they didn't get out of the way of the fires, they would all be dead.

Dai Yue helped her uncle up onto the sidewalk. He staggered forward, then turned to sit down, his back propped against the wall of a residential hotel. The tenants were scrambling in and out of the front door, loading trunks and boxes. One man had a delicately painted delivery wagon advertising a piano-moving company. The horse was exhausted, its head low, almost touching the cobblestones.

Brendan watched Dai Yue sink down beside her uncle. She looked different somehow—younger, more timid. A sudden commotion made Brendan turn and look across the intersection at the far side of Powell Street. A group of men in dark uniforms were standing outside a saloon. A sign advertising Yosemite Lager Beer was painted across the second story. A beautiful mountain scene with pine trees seemed to promise customers more than a glass of beer.

The soldiers were trying to get past the bald man who stood solidly in the doorway. He was shaking his head and the voices became shouts. Brendan could make out part of what they were saying.

" . . . order of the mayor," one soldier yelled, holding his rifle high, threateningly. "We have the authority to . . . "

An automobile full of furniture rumbled past and Brendan couldn't hear for a moment. The driver turned down Clay Street—Powell Street was almost entirely blocked with rubble about half a block up. Once the automobile had passed, Brendan strained to hear the argument again.

"That's trespassing!" the bald man was shouting over and over.

The soldier who seemed to be in charge had stepped back. He had shifted the position of his rifle so the barrel pointed vaguely in the direction of the saloon owner, but still angled toward the ground. Brendan stared. It would take the soldier only a split second to raise his rifle to fire.

" . . . the right to steal a man's property," the bald man was saying. "Who gave you the authority to do that?"

The soldier frowned, replying in a voice too low for Brendan to hear. Then he stepped back one more pace, his eyes never leaving the saloon keeper's. He slowly raised the rifle, holding it steady, aiming at the man's chest. Two of the other soldiers lifted their rifles as well. The others just stood, waiting.

After a few seconds, the bald man moved away from the door. He stood on the curb as the soldiers filed into his establishment. A moment later the first of them reappeared, carrying a heavy whiskey keg. Grunting, he set it on the curb, then went back in.

Brendan glanced back at Dai Yue. She was sitting beside her uncle. He was still leaning back against the building, his eyes closed, his mouth slightly open now. Dai Yue was watching people pass on Clay.

"Let's get this finished up quick!" the officer shouted. Brendan looked back across the street. Working hard, the soldiers had piled ten whiskey kegs and eleven or twelve larger beer barrels in front of the saloon. As Brendan watched, one of them pulled an ax from his pack.

The bald man turned aside as the soldier stood over one of the barrels, raised the ax high over his head, and then swung, his arms rigid with effort. The ax crashed into the oaken barrel. The staves shattered beneath the blow and amber-colored whiskey flowed into the gutter.

Men stopped to gawk as the next barrel, then the next was shattered. The blows of the ax rang out over the murmur of voices. A man called out, demanding to know what the soldiers were doing.

"General Funston has ordered all liquors destroyed or seized, sir," the officer called back. "This city faces enough disorder without public drunkenness making matters worse."

The man nodded grudgingly. Brendan could hear the soldier's words being repeated, the explanation passing through the crowd.

As Brendan turned to face Dai Yue again, the street heaved beneath his feet. The jolt was sharp enough to make him stumble backward. As he caught his balance, he saw a cart horse rearing, its driver dragging at the reins to control it. After a few seconds, the city quieted, then came back to life again once the ground had settled into stillness.

Brendan stood motionless, his heart pounding.

A high-pitched wailing assaulted his ears. At first he had no idea where it was coming from. Then he turned. Dai Yue was screaming.

CHAPTER NINE

Dai Yue stumbled upright and whirled away from her uncle. She did not realize the high-pitched wailing was coming from her own lips until she saw two men looking at her, then the concern on Brendan's face. But even once she realized what she was doing, it took her a moment to stop, to cover her mouth with her hands. Her whole body was shaking.

She stared down at her uncle. She had gripped his hand when the ground started moving. He had not responded. He had not opened his eyes when she called his name. He had not wakened when she had gripped his shoulder. He lay now at a twisted angle, his fall stopped only because he had slumped against the brick wall.

"Dai Yue?" Brendan ran toward her. People in the street were moving again, their eyes fastened on the cobblestones in front of them. "Dai Yue, what's wrong?" Brendan yelled as he came to stand beside her.

She tried to speak but could not. Her thoughts were tangled and would not separate themselves into sense. Her uncle was dead. She knew it. She knew it without touching him, without listening for a whisper of breath, without feeling the warmth drain from his skin.

Brendan was staring into her face, his eyes searching for a wound, a bruise. He held her shoulders. She raised one shaking hand and pointed.

Brendan seemed to understand immediately. He ran to kneel beside her uncle. Dai Yue could not bear to watch as Brendan tried to rouse him. She turned and faced the street. The people passed without so much as a glance. She saw a young mother leading two children, a third in her arms. They were all crying.

"Dai Yue?" Brendan's voice was curt.

She forced herself to face him. Her uncle had fallen sideways. Brendan was struggling to lay him down on his back.

"Help me, Dai Yue."

She shook her head. If her uncle was dead, she had no one, no place to go.

"Help me," Brendan said again. His face was pale, his eyes wide.

Dai Yue shook her head again, but forced herself to take a step toward him. She felt cold suddenly, and her legs seemed to be made of rubber. She saw sparkles floating in the air in front of her and stumbled sideways. Brendan's hands were suddenly on her shoulders. He steadied her until the wheeling sparks receded, then disappeared.

"Dai Yue?"

"Yes?"

"He's dead."

She squeezed her eyes shut. "I know." As soon as she spoke the words, a blackness seemed to swell inside her, pushing its way into her heart. *Alone.* She was alone.

"We have to go."

Dai Yue looked up wildly. What did he mean? She could not leave her uncle to lie in the street like a dog. She would have to arrange a funeral, a banquet for his business associates, for his wealthy clients. She could not dishonor him by—

"We can't stay here. The fires are coming fast."

Dai Yue wrenched free, staggering backward.

Brendan was looking toward Chinatown. "Dai Yue, there's nothing else we can do."

Dai Yue heard his words and she understood them. But the meaning lay on the surface of her thoughts. It did not touch the seething clouds of confusion that raged inside her. She could not leave her uncle here. How could she do that? Her ancestors were whispering to her from their graves. They were angry that she would allow this boy to touch her uncle, to talk about leaving his body in a filthy Fon Kwei street.

"Dai Yue."

He reached for her but she spun away from

him, bumping into a man carrying a crate of frightened doves. The birds fluttered and the man cursed her without really looking at her. She backed away from him, her eyes still on Brendan.

"I won't leave you here."

Dai Yue began to shake. The trembling rose from her legs into her belly and it took a few moments for her to realize that it was not just inside her. The city was quivering again. Bricks fell into the crowd. The soldiers across Powell Street looked up from their spilled liquor and scowled, waiting for the tremor to stop. When it did, Brendan spoke.

"I won't leave you and I can't carry you. You have to come on your own."

Dai Yue met Brendan's eyes. Her home had been in Chinatown, with her uncle, with her people. If she went with this Fon Kwei boy now, her ancestors would not forgive her. They would no longer watch over her bed at night, they would no longer protect her. How could she do such a thing? She sat down beside her uncle and closed her eyes.

★ ★ ★

Brendan stood, astonished. The smoke was so heavy that a false dusk dimmed the streets. He looked longingly down Clay Street in the direction they had been headed. On the horizon there was a patch of blue sky. He took a few steps toward it, then stopped. He glanced back. People were stepping around Dai Yue and her uncle's body, barely glancing down.

Brendan forced himself to walk on. He knew what it felt like to have no one to depend on, no place to call home. It would be even worse for Dai Yue. Not only was her uncle dead, but her home was going to be nothing but ashes. Her people would be scattered and she would be lost and afraid outside of Chinatown.

Turning so quickly that he almost ran into a young couple, Brendan started back. It was hard to see in the smoky light. Coughing, he wove in and out of the mass of people clogging the street and jumped back up onto the sidewalk at the corner.

"Dai Yue!" She looked up at him, her eyes dull. Although there was fire all around them, Brendan could see no light in Dai Yue's eyes. Looking past her Brendan saw that the smoke from Chinatown was darker now. Flames climbed the frame buildings. He reached down and took her hand. She got to her feet, her eyes still dull. But she followed when he led her to the far side of Clay Street. He didn't want her to have to see her uncle's body again.

They walked for nearly a half mile before Brendan loosened his grip on Dai Yue's hand. As they walked, the tall buildings lining Clay Street gave way to smaller businesses, then grand homes that sat in the center of wide lots. They were going uphill now. Brendan kept a careful eye on Dai Yue. She shuffled along, her eyes on the cobblestones.

Brendan kept glancing over his shoulder. As they got farther from the flames, people calmed down a little. He could hear conversations on every side. People were trying to decide where to go.

Brendan glanced at Dai Yue. "I wonder what will happen to everyone." Dai Yue did not answer. Brendan waited, but she didn't even look up at him. "I mean, I wonder if people will rebuild their houses and their shops or if they will just leave San Francisco now."

Dai Yue lifted her eyes. He was never sure how much of what he said she understood. She met his eyes for a moment, then looked aside.

"These were beautiful homes," Brendan said. He gestured.

This time Dai Yue nodded, a motion so slight that he wasn't sure he had really seen it.

As they came up the hill to Post Street they passed three or four palm trees on the right side of the road. An ornate iron fence topped with spikes marked the edge of some rich man's domain.

"I want a house like that someday," Brendan said without thinking. Then he laughed. "Well, I'd prefer it to have more than one wall standing." He looked at Dai Yue out of the corner of his eye. He thought he saw her smile.

The chimneys were still standing upright.

There were four. Brendan tried to imagine a house with even one hearth that grand. It was hard.

"My cousin was houseboy," Dai Yue said suddenly. She pointed down a side street. "Before he die."

Brendan waited, hoping she would say more, but she did not. Still, a little light seemed to be coming back into her eyes. "Your cousin worked in one of these houses?"

Dai Yue ducked her head in a quick nod. "Houseboy."

Brendan just wanted her to keep talking. Anything was better than her silence. He was trying to think of something else to say when explosions from Chinatown made them both turn to look. The flames were flashing from the walls of smoke now. It was hard to tell exactly where the fires were—but they were spreading, growing into a solid line that advanced steadily.

"I not have home."

Brendan heard the desolation in her voice—and he recognized it. "I felt that way when my pa died. But it works out."

Dai Yue turned without speaking and started walking again. Her long trousers were torn and soiled. Although she took small steps, she walked quite fast.

Brendan had to run a little to catch up. "It does get better, Dai Yue. You will start to figure out your own life."

She looked up at him.

"I mean you will decide what you want to do."

Dai Yue shook her head. "I want nothing."

Brendan made his way around a pile of crumbled brick. "You won't feel that way forever."

Dai Yue didn't respond. She began to walk faster. Brendan could feel a little breeze starting up behind them. He glanced back toward the fires. If the wind came up, they would spread even faster. He could see the Fairmont Hotel off to the right. It looked even bigger than it usually did because so many of the buildings that stood around it had collapsed.

Brendan lengthened his stride a little, to keep up with Dai Yue. His legs felt heavy. It was hard to continue putting one foot in front of the other. He tried to swallow, feeling the dryness of his throat and the emptiness of his belly. His hunger was painful.

It had been a long time since he had been this hungry. He hated it. It reminded him of that first awful year after his father had died. He had been nine and scrawny. No one had wanted to hire him. Old man Hansen had caught him going through a trash barrel and had put him to work sweeping floors.

Dai Yue was still walking fast. She looked so sad that Brendan wished he could think of something to say to her. But what? He knew what she was feeling, and he knew that a few words wouldn't help. The bandage on his head had loosened. He unwound it, then touched his temple. The bleeding had stopped. He let the bloody strip of Dai Yue's tunic fall from his hand.

Behind them, a sudden clatter of hooves rang out on the cobblestones. Brendan heard some-one shout, curse. A soldier on horseback was forcing his way through the crowd. He spurred his mount forward as people pushed each other, trying to get out of his way.

When the soldier neared the corner he reined in and dismounted. Brendan watched him pull a sheet of paper and a hammer from a pouch tied to his saddle. Clenching nails in his teeth, he hung the sign from the wooden pole that supported the electrical wires.

Brendan pulled Dai Yue with him as he veered to join the group of men who stood in a loose half circle in front of the notice the soldier was posting.

"This is crazy," a man said from in front of Brendan.

"It makes Schmitz king of the city," another put in.

A third man was shaking his head. "Schmitz is a good mayor. He's only doing what he has to."

The first two men moved away so that others could see. Brendan stepped up, waiting his turn. The soldier was remounting, his horse stamping impatiently, eager to be free of the press of people. Two more men finished reading. Now Brendan could see the notice:

PROCLAMATION
By The Mayor

The FEDERAL TROOPS, the members of the REGULAR POLICE FORCE, and all SPECIAL POLICE OFFICERS have been authorized by me to kill any and all persons found engaged in LOOTING or in the COMMISSION of ANY OTHER CRIME.

I have directed all the GAS and ELECTRIC LIGHTING COMPANIES not to turn on GAS or ELECTRICITY until I order them to do so. You may therefore expect the city to remain in darkness for an indefinite time period.

I request all citizens to remain at home from darkness until daylight every night until order is restored.

I warn all CITIZENS of the danger of fire from DAMAGED or DESTROYED CHIMNEYS, BROKEN or LEAKING GAS PIPES or FIXTURES, or any like cause.

E. E. SCHMITZ, MAYOR
Dated April 18, 1906

"What it says?" Dai Yue asked as Brendan led her back through the people who had gathered around the notice.

"It says the same thing the soldiers were shouting this morning. Anyone who tries to steal will be shot."

"Shot?" Dai Yue looked startled.

Brendan nodded. "Shot. And the streetlights aren't going to come on tonight. It says we are supposed to stay home."

"Home?"

Brendan shrugged. How could people stay home when their houses had been burned to the ground? He began to laugh. It hurt, but he could not stop. Dai Yue was looking at him strangely. He saw a man glance in his direction. But still, he could not stop laughing—until he started to cry. Dai Yue stood beside him, silent, holding his hand. When he could, he pulled in a long breath and they started walking again.

CHAPTER TEN

"Children!"

Dai Yue spun around, recognizing Miss Agatha Toland's voice. She was coming toward them, walking as fast as she could. She was still pulling the child's toy wagon that held the gray parrot's cage. The big bird paced on its perch, tilting its head one way, then the other. It whistled.

Miss Toland stepped toward them. "What are you two doing here all alone?"

Dai Yue looked at Brendan, hoping he would speak for them both. It was so hard for her to find the strange Fon Kwei words in her mind. It was as though they swam away from her, slip-pery and elusive.

"We've just been walking. . . ." Brendan shook his head in wonderment.

Dai Yue saw Miss Toland smile. "I thought I'd go to the camp they're setting up in Lafayette Square until they let me go home. No one seems to know what the fires will do. This whole city is going to be reduced to tents and makeshift shelters in the blink of an eye."

Dai Yue looked at her. Miss Toland's clothing was smeared with dirt. Her hair was still spiky and uncombed. It had gained a thin coating of ash.

"We need to find something to eat," Brendan said.

Dai Yue felt her stomach cramp as she thought about food.

"Come with me," Miss Toland said. "There will be breadlines later in the day, or maybe the soldiers will let me go back home. You would be welcome there."

Dai Yue looked up at her and noticed for the first time how exhausted she looked. The wagon was heavy, the hills were steep, and Miss Toland was not young.

"I appreciate your help with Caruso."

At the sound of his name the gray parrot stretched up, arching his neck. "Caruso is a great singer," he said. Then he tipped his head back and sang a few high, shimmering notes.

Dai Yue touched the bird through the cage bars. It was hard to believe that a creature could make such human sounds.

"I guess we could go to Lafayette Square," Brendan said to Miss Toland.

The old woman smiled and shifted her gaze to Dai Yue. "And you, child? Will you come?"

Dai Yue hesitated, then nodded. She had nowhere else to go. Brendan bent to pick up the wagon handle. Dai Yue positioned herself behind the wagon and together they started off. Miss Toland led the way, her head held high and her dirty ruffled dresssing gown swirling around her feet with every step.

They walked for a long time. Clay Street remained crowded, but there were long stretches without much rubble or fallen brick. The cable car tracks were broken in places. They had to make their way around mud sloughs created by broken water pipes.

Dai Yue's back began to hurt a little from bending over, but she did not straighten. She could feel the Fon Kwei eyes as people noticed her. It had to look strange, she thought. A Chinese girl pushing a wagon pulled by a Fon Kwei boy. The parrot sidled to the back of its cage, studying her as the wagon rolled along.

"I am hungry," she whispered to it. The bird cocked its head, staring at her. "Maybe I eat you." The bird squawked as if it had understood and Dai Yue glanced over the top of the cage at Miss Toland's back, but the old woman did not turn.

"I sorry," Dai Yue apologized to the bird. It paced its perch, pretending not to hear. Dai Yue apologized again, this time speaking in Chinese. "It was only a jest," she explained. "You take everything far too seriously." Dai Yue smiled, enjoying her game of conversation with the bird.

Dai Yue raised her eyes once more, wishing she could speak more of the Fon Kwei language, could share the joke with Brendan. She looked over the top of the birdcage, then past Brendan and past the straight back of Miss Toland. What she saw made her stomach turn cold.

A few blocks ahead, Clay Street ended at the edge of a square. There were hundreds of people already there, swarming like insects over the grass, settling onto the ground beneath the trees. The crowd scared Dai Yue. The Fon Kwei soldiers scared her even more. As she watched, one of them pushed an elderly Chinese man along, saying something that she could not hear.

There were dozens of men in dark uniforms. They carried long-barreled guns and were shouting to each other. Dai Yue could only understand a little of what they said.

"Dai Yue, what's wrong?" Brendan had turned around to look at her. Dai Yue did not remember straightening up, letting go of the wagon. Brendan was gesturing, trying to get her to catch up.

Dai Yue knew that she could not face so many shouting Fon Kwei. She turned and began walking away. She heard Brendan calling her name. She heard Miss Toland asking her where she was going. She endured the curious stares of the people on the sidewalk. But she did not stop. She could not stop.

Brendan felt a surge of anger as Dai Yue walked away. Maybe he should have left her alone in Chinatown. Maybe she couldn't understand him well enough to ever really be his friend.

"Did she tell you where's she going?"

Brendan looked at Miss Toland. "No. I don't know."

"Where is her family?"

Brendan shrugged, his weariness suddenly settling like a weight on his shoulders. "She has no family. Neither one of us does."

There was a little silence before Miss Toland spoke. "Shouldn't you try to bring her back?" Miss Toland took the wagon handle from him and nudged his shoulder lightly. "She shouldn't be alone."

Brendan didn't answer her. She had no idea

what he had already done to keep Dai Yue safe. "Maybe she wants to be."

Miss Toland blinked. "No one wants to be alone, dear boy."

Brendan glanced back toward Dai Yue. She wasn't running, nor was she dodging through the throng of people. She was simply walking, her head lowered, her shoulders hunched.

"The soldiers probably scared her," Miss Toland said.

Brendan nodded. He drew in a long breath. He wasn't sure why, but he knew he couldn't just go on with Miss Toland. "I have to go get Dai Yue."

Miss Toland nodded. "I will be in Lafayette Square. Perhaps we will meet again." She pulled a small cloth purse from her bodice and opened it. She took out a dollar and pressed it into his hand. "Thank you kindly for your help."

Brendan shook his head. "I have no change."

Miss Toland nodded briskly. "I need none."

Without another word she stooped to pick up the wagon handle and started off. Caruso spread his wings and laughed, a sound so human that Brendan had to smile. Then he turned to follow Dai Yue.

Working his way to the side of the street, Brendan went fast enough to keep Dai Yue in sight, but no faster. He wasn't at all sure that she would come back with him, or that he had any right to try to make her. The one thing he knew for certain was that he had never been more tired or more hungry in his life. His lips were cracked and he ran his tongue over them, tasting blood.

"You can't go back that way," a man said, gripping Brendan's shoulders so suddenly that he cried out.

"Let go of me!" Brendan twisted to one side.

The man hung on, forcing Brendan to stand still. "It's suicide to try to get back home now."

Brendan jerked free and took a step backward, staring into the man's eyes. "It's none of your business where I go, mister."

The man shook his head. "What's wrong with you, boy? Can't you tell when someone is trying to help you?"

Brendan didn't answer. He lunged past the

man and ran. Dodging in and out of the crowd, he expected to spot Dai Yue at any second. He ran down a hill, scanning the sidewalk ahead of him. The man was right. Almost no one was heading back toward the fires now.

Brendan slowed to a walk again, his breath heaving and painful. The smoke was thick, and it seemed to get thicker with every step he took. He swerved to miss a dead horse, still tangled in its harness. Someone had unhitched the wagon.

"Food here! Food for sale!"

Brendan stumbled to a stop and looked down a side street. Three heavyset men stood in front of a grocery delivery wagon. People were lining up. Brendan sprinted, then slid to a stop behind the third man in line. He felt in his pocket for the dollar Miss Toland had paid him.

Glancing back at the crowds streaming past on Clay Street, Brendan shifted his weight from one foot to the other, then back. "Hurry up," he whispered under his breath. The man in front of him turned, glaring, then faced front again.

Brendan pressed his lips together. The first man was leaving, carrying a loaf of bread and a can of stew. Brendan's stomach ached imagining how good the stew would taste. The second man took even less time. The third bought only a loaf of bread.

"That'll be a dollar," one of the big men said.

Brendan froze. Had he heard wrong? Mr. Hansen's bread sold for a nickel a loaf. For a second, Brendan stood still, transfixed by the memory of the wagon he had been driving that morning. Where was it now? Was the nervous mare lying dead under a pile of bricks? And who had the bread? Someone like these three men?

Brendan looked at them as the man in front of him pulled coins from his pockets, trying to make the price. These men weren't bakers, and Brendan was willing to bet they weren't delivery boys either. They were too old, and too muscular. They looked like masons or carpenters or—

"You want to buy something, boy? Get out of the way if you don't."

Brendan frowned. "How much is a loaf of bread?"

The man repeated the price. Brendan shook his head. "That's all I have."

"Like I said, boy, make your purchase or get out of the way."

Brendan clenched his fists, too angry to care what happened. "You stole this wagon, didn't you?"

The man only smiled. "You can't steal from the dead, son. Now get back."

Brendan stood his ground for a few seconds, then stepped aside. He made his way back onto Clay Street. There would be other people selling food at more reasonable prices. He began to walk, hurrying, silently cursing himself for stopping. Now he might never find Dai Yue.

CHAPTER ELEVEN

Dai Yue glanced fearfully at the ground as she walked, edging her way around wagons, handcarts, and the endless river of refugees. Day Leong still trembled with rage. She could feel him writhing beneath the cobblestones even now.

Perhaps if she had immediately gone to the temple and prayed, as she should have done, her uncle would be alive. And who else? Had her cousins in Canton been punished as well? Dai Yue stumbled and staggered a few steps before she could catch her balance.

"Look out, stupid girl!"

A heavyset man shoved her aside. Dai Yue fell sideways and for a terrifying moment she lay sprawled on the cobblestones, her cheek pressed again the earth. She could see hundreds of dusty shoes, a horse's hooves, a wagon wheel rolling toward her.

"Get up!"

Dai Yue twisted and found herself looking up at a man on horseback. He was frowning.

"I said, get up. Can you understand me?"

Dai Yue rolled to a sitting position. Her lungs ached, the smoke stinging with every breath. Her temple throbbed. Had she hit her head? She couldn't remember. She felt a warm trickle on her face and for a moment she thought she had begun to cry, but when she tried to wipe away the tears, her fingers came away coated with red.

"Are you hurt? Do you speak English?"

Dai Yue looked up into the face of the soldier. People were streaming around his horse, leaving a bare patch of ground just big enough so no one stepped on her.

"Can you get up or not?" It was a demand, not a friendly inquiry. The soldier looked nervous. He glanced over his shoulder, then back at her. A rifle lay across his saddle. Would he shoot her if she did not get up?

Dai Yue struggled to her feet and stood, swaying. Perhaps the Earth Dragon would writhe again, perhaps the ground would open and she would fall in. Then she would not have to walk another step, would not have to feel the grinding hunger in her belly, would not have to tremble before these Fon Kwei soldiers. The soldier pulled a canteen from his saddle and lifted it to his lips. Watching, Dai Yue swallowed painfully.

"You better find your people," the soldier said roughly. He pulled his horse abruptly to one side and spurred it forward.

Dai Yue stood unsteadily as the flow of people closed in again, like the current in a stream when a rock is moved. She started walking against the crowd again, this time more slowly. She touched her forehead, then looked at her fingers. There was blood, but it was stickier now and she could no longer feel the warm trickle on her cheek.

Working her way to the sidewalk, Dai Yue

found a sheltered doorway and leaned against the brick. She closed her eyes, trying to ease the stinging from the smoke. She stood very still, deliberately slowing her breathing, trying to make sense of her thoughts. She didn't want to go back toward the camp set up by the Fon Kwei solders. But she had no idea where she should go.

Dai Yue opened her eyes and watched people passing. Some were praying, some crying. There were black-skinned people, whites, Chinese, Japanese, and Mexican—and they all looked the same. Most had faces of stone, their eyes empty of everything but weariness and fear.

"Dai Yue!"

She flinched at the sound her name, the familiar voice. Chou Yee pushed his way toward her. His fleshy face was streaked with sweat and ash.

"Dai Yue, where is your uncle?"

She shrank from his touch, shaking her head. "My uncle has died."

Chou Yee took her arm. "Then you must come with me."

Dai Yue freed herself, pressing back against the brick. "I cannot."

Chou Yee frowned. "Of course you can. You must. A girl cannot walk the streets alone. Have you not seen the soldiers?" He took her hand once more. "We will marry soon. You can live in my mother's house until the wedding."

"I do not wish to marry you," Dai Yue said. Her hand flew to her mouth the instant the words came out. She watched Chou Yee's face, terrified, but he only laughed.

"Many girls feel this way. It is quite common. But your uncle and I reached an agreement about this."

"He released me. Just before he died, he said I could marry as I choose."

"This is a Fon Kwei notion. Too many young girls think they know what is best. They do not. You must trust your uncle and trust me."

"I do not want to marry you. I want—"

"Come, we must get away from the fires." He pulled her along, guiding her down the street with an iron grip on her wrist. Dai Yue tried to turn back, but he forced her forward again. "Do you want to die in the flames?"

She shook her head, her eyes on the cobblestones. Of course she did not want to die. Did he think her stupid? She tried to find the courage to tell him that she would not marry him, ever. But her voice was trapped by her fear.

"Come along, Dai Yue!" Chou Yee's anger was apparent in his voice. "I do not wish to drag you every step of the way."

Dai Yue stopped. "I will not go with you."

His face was hard to see. It was close to sunset and the smoke was a dark ceiling hanging low over the city. When she spoke, she felt his hand tighten painfully on her wrist.

"You *will* come with me. And you must stop this arguing. Your uncle arranged our marriage. It is your duty."

Dai Yue shook her head and tried to back away. Chou Yee wrestled with her, cursing. People walked around them, few even noticing their struggle.

"Dai Yue!"

She lifted her eyes to see Brendan coming

toward her. His pale face shone in the dusky light. Dai Yue met his eyes, wondering if he could tell how frightened she was.

"Let her go!" Brendan shouted at Chou Yee.

Chou Yee straightened and turned to face Brendan. He laughed, then spoke in Chinese. "You are a boy. What are you shouting at me?" Chou looked at Dai Yue. "This Fon Kwei boy knows your name. Why?"

Dai Yue saw Brendan's confusion. "This Chou Yee," she said in English.

Brendan blinked. "The man you were supposed to marry?"

"Yes," Dai Yue said.

"But your uncle said you didn't have to. Tell him that. Tell him to let you go."

Dai Yue drew in a long breath and turned to Chou Yee. "This Fon Kwei boy helped my uncle, then asked for one favor—that I be released from our arrangement of marriage. My uncle granted this before he died."

"You are lying," Chou Yee accused.

"Let her go," Brendan repeated. He stood just beyond Chou Yee's reach.

"Let me go," Dai Yue said in Chinese.

Chou Yee jerked her forward, shoving Brendan aside. Dai Yue stumbled, pulling Chou Yee off-balance. She fought against his grip but could not break it.

"Let her go!" Brendan shouted.

Dai Yue glanced back over her shoulder. She saw Brendan pick up a brick, then come forward. She lunged sideways. Chou Yee stiffened, his arm extended almost straight out from his body as he held tight to her wrist.

In that instant, Brendan slammed the edge of the brick across Chou Yee's forearm. Chou Yee screamed and Dai Yue jerked free.

"Run!" Brendan yelled at her, throwing down the brick and racing off.

Dai Yue stumbled forward. The sound of Chou Yee's cursing faded quickly into the din surrounding them, but Brendan did not slow down and Dai Yue tried to keep up with him.

Finally Brendan broke his pace and they walked side by side. For a time Dai Yue's heart was like a freed firefly. Then it began to feel heavy again. The dark was closing in around them. She was dizzy with hunger and thirst.

Brendan turned down a side street. "We need to get back to Lafayette Square."

Dai Yue pictured the soldiers, their hard faces and their rifles. "I not go," she said in English.

Brendan stared into her eyes. "Then we have to find someplace else to go. I don't want to be wandering around after night falls."

Dai Yue let him lead the way. He kept heading uphill, away from the fires. "Are you all right?"

"Yes," Dai Yue murmured. But the truth was she was not all right. She couldn't imagine ever being all right again.

CHAPTER TWELVE

Brendan no longer knew where he was. Still, Dai Yue followed him without question, her hand tight on his. She seemed to trust him, and he was praying that he could find a safe place for them to rest for the night. Maybe in the morning light he would be able to talk her into going back to Lafayette Square.

Along the skyline behind them and off to their right, fires burned. The eerie orange glow ebbed, then flared in the darkness. Sometimes they could hear explosions. Strange hot breezes touched his face, then were gone. The smoke was still bad, but it was a little thinner here.

Brendan's stomach hurt and he wished over and over that he had taken a few loaves of bread from the wagon before the mare had shied and run off. His mouth was so dry that he could barely swallow.

Brendan wondered what street they were on. He had turned off Clay, then turned again, hoping to make sure that Chou Yee couldn't follow them. He had tried to find less crowded streets—now he was afraid that had been foolish. In the dark, the piles of broken brick and shattered windows were menacing. He stumbled over something and felt Dai Yue tighten her grip to steady him.

"I tired." Dai Yue's voice was small and weak.

Brendan nodded but he didn't answer. He had been up since three o'clock that morning, had begun his deliveries at four. He tried to ignore the aching in his belly. He had spent most of his life without enough to eat but, in the last three years, working for old man Hansen, things had begun to change for him.

"Did you see soldiers down past the Crocker Mansion?"

The gruff voice came from the other side of some shattered brickwork. It was so close that Brendan stopped, startled. Dai Yue stood to one side.

"I didn't see any earlier, Elbert. Maybe they won't go up there." This voice was higher, less rough, and there was a hint of an accent that Brendan couldn't place. Brendan could see the flickering of a small campfire. He could smell meat cooking. His stomach cramped.

"You're such a fool. Half the money in this city is up on Nob Hill. You think those rich folks won't demand protection? You haven't got the brains God gave a goose." The gruff voice was derisive, cruel.

"We go," Dai Yue whispered.

"Not yet," Brendan whispered back. He wanted to hear what these men had to say. And he was afraid to attract their attention.

"There are uniforms swarming all over this city," the rough voice said. "But if we're careful, this could still be our chance."

There was a long silence, then the younger man spoke up. "I guess it isn't exactly stealing."

"Hell no," the rasping voice agreed. "They all have their insurance—they won't lose anything. And even if they don't have insurance, it's like that grocery store. You know the fire is just going to take everything anyway."

Dai Yue stepped back, making a scraping sound on the cobblestones. Brendan held his breath. He waited for them to resume their talk, but they did not. He heard one of them moving and stiffened.

"Who's there?" It was the rough voice.

Brendan felt Dai Yue begin to tremble. The men were getting up, walking around the heap of wreckage, coming toward them.

"What are you doing there?"

Dai Yue bolted and Brendan followed half a heartbeat behind her. There were heavy footsteps behind them as they ran. Dai Yue led the way this time, going as fast as she could through the maze of brick and lumber. After a couple of blocks, the sounds of the men's boots on the cobblestones faded. Brendan could hear the quick gasping of her breath when at last they stopped running.

For a long time, they stood silently in the darkness. When Brendan's breath finally slowed, he faced Dai Yue. "We have to find a place to spend the night." He looked around. It was impossible to tell which way the fires would burn. He started forward, too exhausted to try to figure out the best thing for them to do. All he knew was that they had to keep going until they found a safe place to rest.

One block farther on, Brendan saw a small brick building. Like the rest of the buildings they had passed on this street, it looked deserted. He paused in front of it, not sure why this building had caught his attention. The front door was ajar. He took a deep breath to gather his courage, then pulled it open. No one shouted. There was no sound at all from inside.

"Wait for me," Brendan whispered, releasing Dai Yue's hand. He slipped through the opening. There was a subtle odor that Brendan recognized but couldn't place for a moment. When he did, he almost smiled. The room smelled like the library at St. Mary's. Was this a bookstore?

Brendan took one cautious step, then another, feeling his way. When his fingertips brushed a leather binding, he did smile. Books. No one would be likely to try to steal books tonight. He and Dai Yue would be safe here.

"Dai Yue." He said her name so quietly that he thought she might not hear, but a few seconds later she appeared beside him.

"It's a bookstore," he told her. "Try to find somewhere we can sleep."

He heard her move away, then he took another cautious step. The floor was littered with books. He crouched and pushed a few of the heavy volumes along the floor. His hands slid across a thick wool carpet. "Over here, Dai Yue."

She came to stand beside him again. "Here."

Brendan touched a piece of cloth—some garment, a coat or cape. "Feel this carpet," he instructed her, crouching again.

Dai Yue sank to the floor and made a little sound of delight. She began shoving books out of the way. He helped her and within a few minutes they had cleared a space big enough to lie down in. Brendan stretched out, feeling numb.

Dai Yue arranged the cloth over them both. Brendan knew he ought to say something, to tell her not to be afraid. But she turned over, curling up on her side. Brendan listened to her breathing as it slowed and deepened. He closed his eyes and almost immediately felt the tug of exhaustion pulling him toward sleep.

Brendan felt the tremor in the ground and knew he should jump up, get Dai Yue to her feet, prepare to run—but he couldn't. The tremor subsided. Dai Yue did not even stir in her sleep. Brendan relaxed again. Sleep came easily, warm and dark and comforting. The night went on outside the little shop. Brendan slept peacefully, the smoke, the fires, the shouts all erased for a few hours.

A sharp pain in Brendan's wrist jolted him

from sleep. He jerked his hand back and heard a chittering squeak. Rats. He sat up, shoving back the cape. Dai Yue turned wildly, saying something in Chinese.

Rats skittered away, their claws scraping on book covers, the fallen shelves, the empty window frame. Brendan saw five or six of them flow over the windowsill, their fur as dark as the shadows that still filled the corners of the room.

Brendan blinked. It was getting light. Dawn was near. It took him a moment to realize that Dai Yue was crying. Her shoulders shook. He took both of her hands in his and held them tightly, waiting, not sure what else to do.

"I . . . ," Dai Yue began, then had to stop. He watched her face as she struggled for the words. "I . . . hate rats."

Brendan nodded. "So do I. Let's get out of here."

They got to their feet. Brendan felt as though someone had beaten him. Every muscle hurt. His bones seemed to ache. Dai Yue stretched, yawning and wincing.

Back outside, Brendan walked to the corner and turned in a slow circle, trying to orient himself. The fires were closer. A lot closer. The gray dawn sky was shrouded with smoke.

Brendan glanced at Dai Yue. Her eyes looked hollow and one cheek was reddened beneath the cut on her temple. She noticed him looking and turned away. Brendan studied his hands. He was filthy. Dirt outlined his nails in black.

Brendan lifted his eyes, scanning the ruins of the Financial District on the smoke-blurred horizon. All down Market Street the buildings stood in a jagged line, like gapped teeth. Some had fallen in the earthquake, he knew, but it looked like many more had surrendered to the fires.

The Palace Hotel was still standing, he was pretty sure. It was hard to see it from where he stood. He hoped it had made it through the fire. He loved the graceful arched entries and the beautiful chandeliers. He thought he could see the dome of the Call Building through the smoke, too, but it was hard to tell. He tried to see St. Mary's bell tower, but the smoke was just too thick. He wondered where Mr. Malloy was now.

The line of fires was still marching inland. Chinatown was mostly a charred ruin now, with only its western edge still in flames. Brendan glanced at Dai Yue. Did it upset her to think about her uncle? He had seemed like a coldhearted man.

Brendan looked back out over the city. The flames were moving steadily toward Nob Hill. There were fires up by Russian Hill, too. Was the whole city going to burn?

Dai Yue tapped his shoulder. "Where we go?"

Startled out of his thoughts, Brendan pointed. "That's Van Ness up there a couple blocks. We could drop back down to Clay Street. I still think we should go to Lafayette Square."

Dai Yue's face showed the strain of trying to understand his words. She frowned when he was finished. "No soldiers. Please."

Brendan felt his stomach sink. "I don't know where else to go, Dai Yue." She blinked and he could tell that she was fighting tears. "All right. We will stay away from the soldiers if we can."

Brendan knew that they ought to go to Lafayette Square. They had to find help. They had to eat soon. He felt weak and Dai Yue looked pale and worn-out.

A piercing squeak from a nearby doorway made them both turn. A rat sat on the threshold, cleaning one front paw. Its long, bare tail hung in a curve beside it.

Dai Yue turned. "We go now?"

Brendan started walking. He felt worse than he had before he'd slept. His mouth was sticky and dry and his eyes burned. He pulled in a deep breath to see if his lungs still ached from the smoke. The pain was worse than he expected, and he coughed.

"Hungry." Dai Yue said the single word as though nothing else was needed to describe the world. Brendan nodded, understanding her perfectly.

As they got close to Van Ness, Brendan crossed the street and turned left. They walked slowly, not because the rubble was any worse here than it had been in other places—Brendan just couldn't go any faster. He tried scraping his tongue against his teeth to make saliva, but his mouth was so dry it didn't work.

Brendan saw a few people among the ruined buildings. In the gray light and with the air hazed by smoke, they looked like shadows. One man, carrying a box of oranges, darted across the street in front of them. His eyes flickered in every direction as he ran.

Brendan stopped, astonished that he could smell the oranges. He turned to Dai Yue. "Wait here." He started walking, without allowing himself to think about anything. If there had been one box of fruit, there could be more. He imagined the taste of a juicy orange and ran his tongue over his lips.

In what had to have been a storeroom, Brendan came across two more boxes of oranges. They were heavy, but he managed to hoist a crate up and walk with it. He emerged onto the street, a smile lighting his face as he lifted his head to call out to Dai Yue. But before he could utter a sound, the clatter of hooves startled him and he looked up to see a soldier glaring at him.

The man raised his rifle. "Put down that box, junk thief."

CHAPTER THIRTEEN

Dai Yue watched, crouched in a doorway across the street. The soldier dismounted. He kept his rifle ready and spoke to Brendan in a low, threatening voice.

Brendan glanced around and Dai Yue knew that he was looking for her. She wanted to step forward just enough for him to see her, but she was too frightened of the soldier.

"I said get moving," the soldier ordered, so loudly that his voice echoed.

Brendan began walking. The soldier followed him, leading his horse, the rifle never more than a few feet from Brendan's back. Dai Yue slipped out of the doorway and followed. For a long time, she concentrated on keeping up without the soldiers seeing her. She ran from one pile of bricks to the next, slipped from one shadow to another. It was only on the last stretch of cobblestone that she realized where the soldier was taking Brendan.

Dai Yue stopped, her breath coming in little gasps. The square was packed with people and surrounded by soldiers carrying rifles. She crept forward, then stopped again, feeling nothing but the pounding of her heart.

Her uncle had told her many times that the Fon Kwei soldiers would shoot her people like dogs. She had seen her cousin's body after the Fon Kwei had beaten him to death.

She wanted to follow Brendan, to help him if she could. She understood fully the great debt she owed him. He had saved her life, her uncle's life, then had helped to free her from Chou Yee. But still, she was terrified to walk toward the seething mass of Fon Kwei faces.

"Shoot them all. Kill the looters," someone shouted. A ragged cheer went up from the crowd.

Dai Yue forced herself to place one trembling

foot in front of the other. The crowd seemed like a many-headed dragon. It was in just such a place that her cousin had died.

"Line them up right here!" another voice exploded. This time, the cheers were a little louder and lasted a little longer.

Dai Yue was within a few steps of the crowd now. She lowered her eyes and tried to watch only the ground at her own feet. Her heart beat against her ribs and sweat beaded her brow.

A firm hand suddenly clamped down on Dai Yue's arm and she tried to scream, but nothing came from her lips. It was a demon. She knew it. It was her fate to die in a crowd of Fon Kwei.

"Hello, dear," a voice said from behind her. "Are you all right? Where's Brendan?" Dai Yue looked up into the kind eyes of Miss Agatha Toland.

Brendan stood rigidly, fear prickling at his scalp. The soldier seemed to be enjoying this. He let the rifle barrel brush against Brendan's shirt as they walked. And once they were stopped, facing Lafayette Square, the soldier jabbed him between the shoulder blades, then once in the small of his back.

"Junk thief?" An officer snapped out the question. Then he seemed to really look at Brendan. "He's just a boy."

"Funston's orders don't state an age limit, do they, sir?"

The officer was silent for a moment. "You have a point. Take him over with the other three. Talk to Sergeant Grant."

"Let's go, boy." The rifle dug into Brendan's back once more. He stumbled forward, fear weighting his legs, making him clumsy. He had known that he shouldn't steal the oranges. He had just been so hungry and thirsty he hadn't been able to think clearly. It wasn't an excuse, he knew, but he hadn't meant to steal exactly. His eyes flooded and he forced back the tears. He was not going to cry.

"You have anything to say for yourself, boy?"

Brendan heard the officer's question and turned to face him. The soldier saluted his superior, then stepped back, the rifle still raised and ready.

Brendan squared his shoulders. "I have a dollar. If St. Mary's is still standing, I have more than that. I would be glad to pay anyone for the oranges."

Sergeant Grant glanced past him at the soldier. "He had a box of oranges, sir. Was practically running with them," the soldier barked out.

Brendan hung his head. It was true. The soldier lifted his rifle again and said, "Look a man in the eye when you're talking, boy."

Brendan raised his head to meet Sergeant Grant's steady gaze. "I was just hungry."

"You wouldn't have gone on down the block, looking for jewelry or some poor woman's silver tea service?" Sergeant Grant asked.

Brendan shook his head. "No sir, I would not." He looked directly into the officer's eyes. "I work. I've supported myself since I was nine and my father died. I never took a dime I didn't earn."

"If you need a character witness to confirm that, I'll be honored." Brendan turned at the familiar and welcome sound of Mr. Malloy's voice.

Sergeant Grant cleared his throat. "You know this boy, Mr. Malloy?"

"Everyone on Market Street knows this boy and thinks well of him," Mr. Malloy said.

"Good enough for me," Sergeant Grant responded. "But I can't just release a boy his age back onto the streets. Does he have a family? A guardian?"

"Only me." Brendan watched as Miss Toland stepped out of the crowd, her head held high. Dai Yue was standing next to her.

"Are you his guardian?" the officer asked.

"I am Miss Agatha Toland, officer. You have heard of my family, haven't you?"

Sergeant Grant smiled. "Yes, ma'am, I sure have."

"Then you wouldn't question my intent, would you?"

The officer shook his head. "Of course not, Miss Toland." He looked at Brendan. "All right," he said finally. "But if I see you again before order is restored, it won't end this way."

The officer turned on his heel and Brendan watched him walk away. The soldier lowered the gun, his face expressionless as he followed Sergeant Grant.

"Thank you, sir," Brendan said to Mr. Malloy.

"I'm just glad I was here, boy. With any luck General Funston can figure out how to feed this city before the soldiers shoot half the populace."

Brendan dragged in a deep breath. "I've been thinking about that job, sir, if you meant what you said."

"I meant it," Mr. Malloy assured him. "Just stay with Miss Toland. She's a fine lady. When the city quiets down, you come find me."

Brendan nodded. "I will, sir. And thank you again." Mr. Malloy tipped his hat, then strode away, heading toward the crowds in Lafayette Square, clipboard in hand.

"The first thing we have to do is to get you two some breakfast," Miss Toland was saying. "If we hurry we won't have to stand in line more than an hour or so. With luck, by tonight, we'll all be back in my house." She gestured at the wagon. "Caruso likes sleeping outside, but I don't."

Brendan grinned at her. He didn't mind standing in line. Right now, he didn't mind anything. He looked up at the sky. The smoke had thinned to the west. He could see tiny patches of blue sky. It was going to be a beautiful day. He held out his hand and Dai Yue took it, smiling.